THE CASE OF THE
GREEN-EYED SISTER

THE CASE OF THE
GREEN-EYED SISTER

A PERRY MASON MYSTERY

ERLE STANLEY GARDNER

MYSTERIOUSPRESS.COM

INTEGRATED MEDIA
NEW YORK

Copyright © 1953 by Erle Stanley Gardner

Cover design by Ian Koviak

ISBN: 978-1-5040-6135-3

This edition published in 2020 by MysteriousPress.com/Open Road Integrated Media, Inc.
180 Maiden Lane
New York, NY 10038
www.mysteriouspress.com
www.openroadmedia.com

FOREWORD

Some twenty-eight years ago Ralph Turner, then a young lad of nine, started reading the adventures of Sherlock Holmes and determined that he was going to become a detective.

Several million other young lads, inspired by the same literature, were reaching the same decision.

Ralph Turner's case was interesting for two reasons. First, he was handicapped by a very great speech impediment. He stuttered so badly it was difficult for him to carry on any kind of a conversation. The other interesting thing about Ralph Turner's ambition is that buried somewhere in his character was the quiet, dogged determination that held him steadfast in his decision.

In discussing his career with friends, Ralph Turner casually mentions that "in those days there was no such thing as Police Science as it is taught today." What he neglects to state is the fact that the reason Police Science is being taught today is in a very large measure due to his own quiet, unobtrusive, ceaseless efforts.

Ralph started out to study chemistry with the sole goal of learning how chemistry could aid in the detection of crime. These studies laid the foundation for his textbook, published by Charles C. Thomas in 1949, *Forensic Science and Laboratory Technics.*

This young man who stuttered decided that he had to get rid of his speech impediment in order to carry on his chosen career. His methodical approach to the problem was characteristic of everything he does. He investigated and found that the science of psychoanalysis might offer some hope. He submitted himself to psychiatric treatment, and not only cured his stuttering so that today he is in great demand as a lecturer, but learned enough about psychoanalysis to broaden his understanding of character and motivation—invaluable assets in his chosen field.

In the vanguard of every new movement there are two types. One is the inspired leader, who pioneers the ideas, whose visions would remain only dreams unless they could be implemented by practical, down-to-earth detail work. The other type is the quiet, self-effacing individual, who is usually appointed secretary and plunges into the terrific mass of detail, the extent of which is seldom realized even by close associates.

The pioneer visionary is long remembered. The detail man is referred to as "Good old So-and-So" and the general public never knows he exists.

Ralph Turner is a rare combination. He has inspirational ideas, but he also has that ability to soak up detail, and, by some process of mental alchemy, transform those details into solid, substantial progress.

Slowly but surely progress in the field of Police Science is advancing the technique of investigative work, bringing about higher standards and greater efficiency.

Today the young man who wants to specialize in investigative work finds several colleges offering courses in Police Science.

This newly developed field of study is as important in the field of justice as is legal medicine.

The steady march of science has made tools available for the investigator if he but knows where to find those tools and how to use them. Too often jurors are called upon to rely on surmise or conjecture when, with proper investigative techniques, they could have been presented with solid, substantial proof.

Ralph Turner was made secretary of the American Academy of Forensic Sciences when that organization was brought into existence, and has held the job ever since. He is an associate editor of the *Journal of Criminal Law, Criminology and Police Science.* He is associate editor of the *American Lecture Series in Public Protection.* He is an associate professor in the Police Administration Department of Michigan State College; and for the past five years he and the well-known Dr. C. W. Muehlberger have directed a research project on the reliability of chemical tests for intoxication, the results of which will shortly be published by the National Safety Council Committee on Tests for Intoxication.

But Ralph Turner's progress in his life's work cannot be measured by any listing of academic degrees any more than by spectacular excursions into the field of the dramatic in forensic battles. Ralph Turner's value lies in his ability to create an enthusiasm which the other person feels was entirely self-inspired.

Where other men, temperamental leaders, insist upon recognition or they won't play, Ralph Turner is always willing to subordinate his own individuality, to take on the thankless job of wrestling with endless details in order to advance the cause.

Too frequently such men escape public recognition. The men who are in the limelight know and appreciate their indebtedness to these men, but the public never shares this knowledge. Because I want my readers to know something of this new field which is known as Police Science, and because I want to make a public acknowledgment of the outstanding work that has been so quietly, so faithfully performed by a man who has never been afraid of detail nor known what it is to shirk a responsibility, I dedicate this book to my friend:

Ralph F. Turner

—Erle Stanley Gardner

THE CASE OF THE
GREEN-EYED SISTER

CHAPTER 1

Della Street, Perry Mason's confidential secretary, handed the lawyer a scented, engraved oblong of pasteboard.

"If you're going to do anything for this woman," she said, "you'd better get a retainer."

"In other words, you don't like her?" Mason asked.

"I didn't say that."

"But you don't?"

"I think she'd cut your heart out for thirty-seven cents, if that's what you mean."

Mason studied the card. "Sylvia Bain Atwood," he read aloud. "Miss or Mrs., Della?"

"She's Mrs. Atwood and her green eyes are as cold as a cash register," Della Street said. "Her manner, on the other hand, is a purely synthetic attempt to belie the expression of her eyes. I imagine her whole life has been like that."

"What does she want?"

"It's a business matter," Della Street said, her voice mimicking the mincing manner of the client. "A matter too complicated to be discussed except with a trained legal mind."

"Like that, eh?" Mason asked.

"Exactly like that," she said. "Very hoity-toity. Very snooty. Very superior. Very, very definitely moving in a different social stratum from that occupied by secretaries."

Mason laughed. "Well, send her in, Della."

"She'll turn those green eyes on you," Della warned, "and start twisting and squirming like a cat getting ready to rub against your leg."

Mason laughed. "Well, you've given me a pretty good description of a client whom I don't think I'm going to like. Let's have a look at her, Della."

Della Street returned to the outer office and escorted Sylvia Bain Atwood into Mason's presence.

The green eyes flickered upward in one swift appraisal, then the lids lowered demurely.

"Mr. Mason," she said, "I really feel diffident about approaching you with a problem as simple and as small as mine, but my father always said in dealing with professional men get the best. The best is *always* the cheapest."

"Thank you for the compliment," Mason said, taking her outstretched hand. "Please be seated. Tell me what I can do for you."

Once again the green eyes flashed in swift appraisal, then Mrs. Atwood settled in the client's comfortable chair. A coldly hostile glance at Della Street plainly showed her annoyance at the presence of a secretary. Then she twisted about in the chair in a peculiarly feline manner and adjusted herself into the most comfortable position.

"Go on," Mason said, "tell me what you want. I'll let you know if I'm in a position to be of help, and don't mind Miss Street. She stays and keeps notes on my interviews, puts them in a confidential locked file, and helps me remember things."

"My problem is very simple," Mrs. Atwood murmured deprecatingly.

Mason, catching Della Street's eye, let his own twinkle in amusement. "Then I dare say, Mrs. Atwood, you won't need me," he said. "I'm quite certain if it's such a simple problem you would do better to consult some attorney who is less busy than I am and who would consequently—"

"Oh no, no, no, no, no!" she interrupted quickly. "Please, Mr. Mason! It's—well, I mean it will be simple for *you,* but it might puzzle anyone else."

"Suppose you tell me what it is," Mason said.

"It concerns my family," she said.

"You're a widow?"

"Yes."

"Children?"

"No."

"Then your family?" Mason asked.

"Consists of my sister, Hattie Bain; my brother, Jarrett Bain, his wife, Phoebe; my father, Ned Bain, who is at present confined to his room in the house. He has heart trouble and is required to have absolute rest and quiet."

"Go on."

"*I* am naturally the adventurous type, Mr. Mason." She raised her eyes to his provocatively.

"Go on."

"Hattie is the stay-at-home type. I was always the venturesome one. Hattie stayed to take care of the family. I married. Then my husband died and left me with a not inconsiderable amount of property."

"And then you returned to live at home?"

"Good heavens no! I find the home atmosphere a little—well, a little confining. I have to live my own life. I have an apartment here in town, but I am very fond of my family and I do keep in close touch with them."

"Your mother?" Mason asked.

"She died about a year ago. She'd been sick for a long time."

Della Street glanced at Mason. Mason pursed his lips, thoughtfully regarded Sylvia Atwood.

"Who took care of your mother during her long illness?" he asked.

"Hattie. I don't see why she didn't hire a nurse, but Hattie wouldn't listen to it for a minute. Hattie had to do it all herself. She is the domestic one, the—well, I shouldn't say this, Mr. Mason, but she's the drudge type, the steady-going type."

"And probably a very good thing for your mother that she was."

"Oh, of course," Sylvia agreed readily enough. "She was wonderful to Mother. The point is that I loved Mother just as much as Hattie, but I couldn't have done all that detail work of taking care of her. I'd have stripped myself of all my possessions, if necessary, to have hired nurses, but I'd simply have died if I'd tried to stay home and do the nursing myself."

"I see," Mason observed dryly.

"I'm not certain that you do."

"Does it make any difference?"

"No."

"Then go on and tell me about the matter that's bothering you."

"I'm afraid, Mr. Mason, that I'm dealing with persons who may not be entirely honest."

"What do they want?"

"Money."

"Blackmail?"

"Well, if it is, it's so skillfully disguised that you could hardly call it that."

"Suppose you tell me about it."

"To start with, it goes back to a period several years ago. Texas oil was beginning to be a factor in the life of the state."

Mason nodded encouragement.

"My father had gone broke in the real-estate business. He at that time knew a very peculiar character by the name of Jeremiah Josiah Fritch."

"Quite a name," Mason said.

"They call him J.J., after his first initials."

Mason nodded.

"J.J. had some money. My father had an option on a huge tract of land that he thought might have oil on it, although it was pretty well out of what was then regarded as the oil belt.

"J.J. agreed to buy the land for my father and Dad would put in all of his money in a test well at a point to be designated by J.J."

"That was done?"

"Yes."

"What happened?"

"It was a dry hole. My father still had hope and faith. No one else did. The property naturally declined in value. Dad mortgaged everything he had to J.J. for an option on the property. He secured a new loan from outsiders that were interested in adjoining property and were glad to have Dad exploring the formations. He put down a new well, this time at a spot where he felt there was oil, although J.J. just laughed at him and called the new drilling project 'Bain's Folly.'"

"What happened to that oil well?"

"It opened up a whole new pool. People said it was just luck. They said Dad was trying to tie in on another anticline but stumbled on a new pool. Anyhow, Dad was able to pay off all his loans and buy the property from J.J. and more than recoup his losses."

Mason nodded.

"But the foundation of the whole thing," she said, "was this money J.J. gave Dad."

"Wasn't it a loan?"

"Not exactly. Dad and he were friends. J.J. had other interests. At the start it was a sort of partnership. The point is, Mr. Mason, that all of the money in the family grew out of this original arrangement with J.J. Fritch."

"That is important?" Mason asked.

She nodded.

"Why?"

"Because it now appears that J.J. was a bank robber. Did you ever hear of the spectacular bank robbery known as the Bank Inspector Robbery?"

Mason shook his head.

"A few years ago it was quite famous. A man with elaborately forged credentials as a bank examiner entered one of the big banks.

He managed to get all the cash reserves in a readily accessible place. He also managed to disconnect the emergency alarm that would signal a holdup.

"Then two confederates entered the bank, held up the employees and calmly made off with half a million dollars in cash and traveler's checks."

"Are you trying to tell me that this holdup has some connection with your problem?" Mason asked.

"Exactly. The bank thinks J.J. was one of the gang and that the money he gave Dad was part of the loot."

"Your father wasn't one of the robbers?"

"No, of course not. But they might try to claim he was aware of the fact that the money had been stolen and thereby became a trustee, and in that way the bank could take over the oil lands."

"The bank is claiming that?"

"The bank *may* be *going* to claim that. Apparently—now I'm not able to verify this, Mr. Mason—but apparently as a result of a steady, conscientious search the authorities were able to check the thumbprint of J.J. Fritch on his driving license as being that of the spurious bank examiner."

"After all these years," Mason said.

She nodded.

"How do you know this?"

"From a man by the name of Brogan."

"Who is Brogan?"

"George Brogan, a private detective."

Mason's eyes narrowed. "This sounds like a racket, and I don't think I've ever heard of George Brogan."

"Well, he's an investigator, and I understand his reputation isn't *too* savory."

"It begins to look like an unusual type of blackmail," Mason said.

"So," she said, "if the bank could establish the identity of that money and prove that my father had knowledge, they would then be able to grab our property by claiming that my father had become an involuntary trustee or something of that sort. It's a legal matter, it's complicated and I don't know too much about it."

"The bank has made some effort to do this?"

"No, but I understand from Mr. Brogan that the bank will do it if it has certain information which it may get at any time."

"Tell me more about Brogan."

"Well, Mr. Brogan wants us to understand he definitely is *not* representing J.J. Fritch."

"Where is Fritch?"

"He's not available."

"You mean he's in hiding?"

"Not exactly. He's 'not available' is the way Mr. Brogan expresses it."

"And what does Fritch want?"

"He wants money."

"How much money?"

"A lot."

"That's a typical blackmail setup."

"I can understand that it certainly looks like blackmail."

"What," Mason asked, "specifically is the present situation?"

"George Brogan wants us to employ him to try and work out a solution."

"How much money does *he* want?"

"He says that he'll charge a nominal fee, but that J.J. is badly in need of money and that while he scorns J.J.'s morals, the only way we can be safe is to be certain J.J.'s testimony isn't unfavorable."

"And what do you propose doing?"

"I propose to pay whatever is necessary."

"Why?"

"Because it affects the entire family—not only the money involved but there's the question of the family reputation."

"You must have something more than this to go on," Mason said. "There's something that you haven't disclosed."

"George Brogan has a tape recording."

"Of what?"

"Of what is supposed to be a conversation between J.J. and Dad."

"When did this conversation take place?"

"About three years ago."

"How does it happen that Brogan has this tape recording?"

"Apparently Fritch trapped Dad into the conversation. It took place in Fritch's office and he had a tape recorder."

"Have you heard this tape recording?"

"I've heard part of it. He would only let me listen to just a few words."

"Is it a genuine recording?"

"It sounds like Dad's voice."

"Is it?"

"I don't know."

"Why?"

"Because I've been afraid to ask Dad. In his present condition I wouldn't want to do anything that would disturb him."

Mason nodded to Della Street. "Ring up the Drake Detective Agency," he said. "Get Paul on the phone."

"No, no, please!" Sylvia Atwood exclaimed. "Not another private detective. I detest them."

"Drake is an ethical detective," Mason said. "I have to contact him because I want to find out about Brogan."

Della Street's swift fingers dialed a number on the private unlisted trunk line which was on her desk and which detoured the switchboard in the outer office.

A moment later, when she had Paul Drake on the line, she nodded to Mason.

Mason picked up the extension phone on his desk, said, "Paul, this is Perry. I want to find out something about a George Brogan who seems to be a licensed private investigator. Do you know anything about him. . . . You do, eh. . . . All right, let me have it."

Mason listened for nearly a minute, then said, "Thanks, Paul. I may be calling you in connection with a case."

He hung up the telephone.

Sylvia Atwood's green eyes were intent with an unspoken question.

"Well," Mason said, "Brogan is quite a character. He drives an expensive automobile, maintains a membership in a country club and a yacht club, has a swank apartment, has been under fire three or four times over a question of losing his license, and no one seems to know just how he makes his money."

"Does he make professional contacts at his country club?" she asked.

Mason said, "According to my sources of information, the people who know him would be the last ones to give him business."

"In other words, your detective tells you that he's a high-class blackmailer."

Mason grinned. "If he'd told me that I wouldn't tell you."

"Well, *I'm* telling it to *you* then."

Mason said, "Of course, as between an attorney and client, it's a privileged, confidential communication, but I still wouldn't say it."

"And wouldn't admit that that was what your friend, Mr. Drake, had told you."

Mason grinned, shook his head.

"You mentioned a relationship of attorney and client," she said. "I hope that means that you are going to accept me as a client."

"And, to make it official," Mason said, "you're going to pay me a retainer of five hundred dollars, because when I take my next step I don't want to have any misunderstanding about whom I'm representing and what I'm trying to accomplish."

"What's going to be your next step?"

Mason merely held out his hand.

"Surely," she said, "I don't carry five hundred dollars in cash in my purse."

"Your check's good."

She hesitated for a moment. Her green eyes were hard and appraising, then she opened her purse, took out a checkbook, and wrote Mason a check.

Mason studied the check carefully, then said, "Put on the back of it, 'As a retainer on account of legal services to be rendered.'"

She wrote as Mason suggested.

Mason blotted the check, handed it to Della Street, who placed a rubber stamp endorsement on it.

Mason pulled the telephone toward him, said, "You want me to handle this my own way?"

"I want results."

Mason said to Della Street, "Look up the number of George Brogan, Della. Get him on the line. We'll place that call through the switchboard."

"Do you think it's wise for you to talk with Mr. Brogan?" Sylvia Atwood asked.

"Somebody has to talk with him."

"*I've* already talked with him."

"I don't think it's wise for *you* to continue to talk with him."

"He assures me that he's just trying to be helpful, that every cent of money he receives will be accounted for, that he'll have to pay it over to Fritch in order to hold him in line."

"And in the meantime," Mason said sarcastically, "Fritch has given him possession of the spool of tape containing the recording of the conversation supposed to be between your father and Fritch?"

She nodded.

"Does that impress you as being a little unusual?"

"Well, of course, J.J. would have to do something in order to turn his information into money."

Della Street nodded to Perry Mason.

Mason picked up the telephone, said, "Hello. Brogan, this is Perry Mason. I want to see you. . . . It's about a matter in which I've been retained by Sylvia Bain At-wood. . . . That's right. . . . I want to hear the recording. . . . No, I want to hear it all, every bit of it. . . . Why not. . . . Well, you can't expect so much as a thin dime. . . . All right, tell Mr. Fritch that he can't expect even a thin dime unless I hear all of that recording and unless I'm satisfied it's an authentic recording. . . . To hell with that stuff. Tell your friend, Fritch, that he's dealing with a lawyer now. . . . All right, if he isn't your friend, the message is still the same. . . . That's right, every bit of recording that's on that tape. . . . Every word. . . . Otherwise Fritch can go roll his hoop. . . . When I advise a client about buying a horse I want to see the horse, all of it. . . . That's right.

"When. . . . I can't. I'm going to be busy in court. . . . All right, then make it right away. I'll be over within ten minutes. . . . Why not. . . . All right, at your apartment then. I don't care. . . . An hour. . . . All right."

Mason hung up the telephone, said to Sylvia, "I'm going over to Brogan's apartment. I'm going to hear that recording. I'm going to hear all of it. You'll have to be there with me. I want you to listen carefully and tell me if you feel the voice you hear on the recording is that of your father. Now I'm going to tell you something else. I don't like blackmail."

"You think this is?"

"It's first cousin to it," Mason said. "It smells like blackmail, and it's an aroma I don't care for. Now I want you to do one other thing for me."

"What?"

Mason said, "When I go over there I'm going to wear a hearing aid. I'm going to pretend to be a little deaf. I want you to play up to me on that."

"Why the hearing aid?"

"Perhaps," Mason said, grinning, "because I want to hear better. Now we're to meet him at his apartment in an hour. I want you to meet me here in forty-five minutes. It'll take us about fifteen minutes to get to his apartment from here. In the meantime I don't want you to say anything to anyone about what we're doing."

She nodded.

"Now then," Mason went on, "suppose it turns out this is a genuine recording of a conversation that actually took place between your father and J.J. Fritch, and in that conversation your father admits in effect that he knew the money used by Fritch in the partnership deal was the proceeds of a bank robbery. What are you going to do?"

"We're going to pay off unless you can find some better way of handling it."

"How much are you going to pay?"

She hesitated. Her eyes avoided his.

"How much?" Mason asked.

"As much as he demands, if we have to."

"And then what?"

"And then I want to be very, very certain that there isn't any more proof, that all of the proof is in our hands."

"How do you propose to do that?"

"I don't know. That's why I came to you. I thought I'd leave that up to you."

Mason said, "You can take a spool of recorded tape and dub a dozen different duplications if you want to. If they're well made on good equipment those duplications will be just as faithful as the original."

"Mr. Brogan says he'll guarantee J.J.'s good faith in the matter, that there is only one recording, that no copies have been made."

"Just how does he propose to guarantee that?"

"I don't know. He said we could depend on his word."

"Do you think his word's any good?"

She said pointedly, "I gave you five hundred dollars, didn't I? That's the best answer I can make."

"I thought so," Mason said. "It's a mess. We'll try and handle it the best we can."

"And I'm to be back here in forty-five minutes."

"Forty minutes now," Mason told her. "On the dot."

"Very well." She arose and left the office.

When the door had clicked shut behind her Della Street raised questioning eyes at Mason.

Mason said, "First, I'm going to find out whether that's her father's voice or not. I'm going to prove that much to my own satisfaction."

"How?"

"I'm going to listen to that recording and I'm going to keep on listening to it until I'm fully familiar with the voices, then I'm going to make it a point to see Ned Bain. I'll talk with him about the weather or anything else. I'll study his voice and compare it with the voice on the recording, and I'll have a scientific comparison made. We'll slow the recording down and we'll slow down recordings of Bain's voice. We'll speed them up. We'll make every scientific comparison we can."

"But I don't see how you'll have any opportunity to make all those examinations of the voice on the record. Do you think Brogan will let you take the record to play with, or make a copy of it?"

Mason grinned. "You haven't heard about my affliction."

"What?"

"About being deaf."

Mason opened the drawer of his desk, took out a small, oblong metal container which he slipped into his side coat pocket, then he clipped a device which held a small microphone up against the bone of his head just over the right ear.

"All right," Della Street said, "that may help you to hear more distinctly, but how is it going to help you study what's on that tape recording?"

Mason said, "Of course, I'll conceal the wires, running them in through a hole in my coat pocket and up through the shoulder of the coat."

"But I still don't see," Della Street protested.

Mason reached in the drawer of his desk, took out a small compact extension speaker about four inches in diameter. He placed that on his desk, plugged it into the flat device in his pocket and flipped a switch.

Della Street heard her own voice, startlingly lifelike, say, "All right, that may help you to hear more distinctly, but how is it going to help you study what's on that tape recording?"

Mason grinned as he saw the expression of utter consternation on Della Street's face. He disconnected the loud-speaker and put it back in the drawer of his desk.

"Good heavens!" Della Street said. "How did you do that?"

"This little device," Mason said, "is of German manufacture. It makes a wire recording for two and half hours on wire that is so small it is all but invisible except under a microscope. When there is no interference it gives an astonishing fidelity of tone reception. While I am listening to that recording over in Brogan's apartment I'll actually be making a copy of it that we can experiment with."

"How do you get the power for that?" Della Street asked.

"Batteries and tubes," Mason said. "Just the same as with a pocket radio set or with a hearing aid."

"Suppose Brogan finds out what you're doing?"

"He won't."

"But suppose he does."

"All right," Mason said, "what can he do?"

"He could—well, he could become very disagreeable."

"So can I," Mason told her, grinning.

CHAPTER 2

Mason entered the office of the Drake Detective Agency.

"Paul in?" he asked the receptionist.

She nodded.

"Busy?"

"On the telephone is all. I'll tell him you're coming."

She plugged in a line, flashed a signal, then nodded to Mason. "Go right on down."

Mason opened a latched gate in a waist-high partition, walked down a long corridor which contained a veritable rabbit warren of offices on each side, small cubbyholes for the most part, where operatives could make their reports.

Paul Drake's office was at the far end of the corridor. Drake was talking on the phone as Mason entered.

He motioned Mason to a seat, finished his telephone conversation, hung up and turned to grin at the lawyer.

Mason seated himself in an uncushioned wooden chair, regarded the detective across a desk which was decorated with half a dozen separate telephones.

"It's a wonder you wouldn't get a decently comfortable chair for clients," Mason said.

"Then they'd stay too long," Drake told him. "I can't charge whopping big fees the way a lawyer can. I have to carry on a volume of business. Right now I have a dozen cases going, with men out working on those cases, phoning in reports, asking for instructions. Why were you inquiring about Brogan? You aren't getting mixed up with him, are you?"

Mason took a cigarette case from his pocket, snapped it open, offered Drake a cigarette.

The detective, tall, languorous, his face carefully schooled to an expression of disinterest, stretched forth a lazy hand, extracted a cigarette, snapped a match into flame.

"You tangle up with Brogan," he went on, "and you'll learn something about the noble art of shakedown."

"I'm tangled with him," Mason said.

"In that case you'd better let Della keep all of your money for you until you get untangled."

"What's wrong with him, Paul?"

"Everything."

"You weren't too emphatic over the telephone."

"I try to be a little cautious over the telephone. I gave you the sketch, however."

"What about him?"

"Well," Drake said, "for one thing he's a blackmailer. They can't catch him at it, but he's a blackmailer."

"Why can't they catch him at it?"

"Because he's too damn clever. He never appears as a black-mailer. Apparently *he* never gets any part of the money that's paid over as blackmail, but you let Brogan get hold of a piece of confidential information and sometime within the next year or eighteen months, after no one would think of connecting it up with George Brogan, some blackmailer will approach Brogan and demand that Brogan's client pay a shakedown.

"Brogan, of course, will immediately get in touch with his client. Brogan will be completely dismayed. He'll accuse the client of having let the cat out of the bag. The client will assure him that the information Brogan had was completely confidential. Brogan will start cross-examining the client, asking him if he didn't tell some-one, if he didn't tell his wife, if he didn't tell his sweetheart, if his secretary didn't know about it, if he didn't confide in his income-tax accountant or if he hadn't told someone at the club.

"Of course, the answer is always the same. During an eighteen-month period a man will have told *someone*. If he hasn't, Brogan will make him think he has. Then Brogan will be employed to settle the deal with the blackmailer.

"Brogan will look into the thing and advise the client that about the only thing he can do is to make a payoff; that Brogan, by reason of his reputation and his underworld connections, can manipulate things so that the payoff will only be about half what it would otherwise be, and he promises that he can fix things so there will only be one payoff; that he'll not only get the evidence but he'll put fear into the heart of the blackmailer so that there won't be any recurrence, any comeback, there won't be any question of a sucker being bled until he's white."

"And then what?" Mason asked.

"Then the sucker pays Brogan about half the amount of money that the blackmailer has first demanded, according to Brogan. That money disappears. Brogan turns the evidence back to the sucker and charges the sucker a fee, which is usually very nominal under the circumstances."

"And what becomes of the blackmail money?"

"Brogan gets the bulk of it," Drake said, "but you can't prove it. They've tried to prove it half a dozen different times, but they've never been able to tag Brogan with anything. He's smart."

"How smart?"

"Plenty smart, in a slimy sort of way."

"And what happens when there's a comeback, when they start bleeding the sucker white?"

"That's the point," Drake said. "That's where Brogan gets by. They don't do it. When you're dealing with Brogan it's once on the line and that's all. He makes good on that. He claims that he puts fear into the heart of the blackmailer so that nothing happens. Actually, of course, he's in on the racket all the way through, but I couldn't tell you that over the telephone where you might repeat it to a client. I wouldn't dare to say it to anyone else."

Mason said, "It looks as though I'll have an interesting session with him."

"When?"

"In about twenty minutes. I'm to meet him at his apartment."

"Watch your step, Perry."

"I'm watching it," Mason said. "Now here's what I want you to do, Paul. You know Brogan."

"You mean personally?"

"Yes."

"Sure."

"You can describe him?"

Drake nodded.

"Do you have some operatives who know him personally?"

"I can probably get some. How much time do I have?"

"Not very much. Fifteen or twenty minutes."

Drake said, "You always want something in a rush."

Mason grinned. "You get paid for it, don't you?"

Drake nodded.

Mason said, "I have an appointment with Brogan at his apartment. Now I want a couple of operatives stationed at the door of that apartment house. I want men who know Brogan if possible. Otherwise I want you to give them a detailed description of Brogan. After I leave, Brogan is going to go some place, probably in a hurry. I want him shadowed. I want to know where he goes. I want to know with whom he talks. And if he talks with a man by the name of Fritch I want an operative to take over and shadow Fritch."

"Okay," Drake said, reaching for the telephone. "Can do."

Drake picked up the telephone, gave instructions to his secretary to have two operatives whom he named get in touch with him immediately. He dropped the telephone back into place, said to Mason, "What kind of a deal is it?"

"It's a deal involving a tape recording of a conversation," Mason said. "I think the tape recording is probably a phony, I don't know. But I'm going up there to listen to it. Brogan claims that he knows nothing whatever about that tape recording except that a man by the name of J.J. Fritch came to him and told him he had this tape recording, that it would completely ruin a family by the name of Bain, that it would wipe out extensive property holdings, that Fritch needed money, that he was going to force Bain to pay him that money, otherwise he'd use the tape recording in such a way that Bain would be ruined. Then Fritch, believe it or not, entrusted this tape recording to Brogan.

"Brogan apparently was very much shocked. He went to a representative of the family, a woman who has money, told her about it and asked her what she wanted to do. He said that she could count on him to do anything she wanted except that he couldn't destroy the tape recording because he had given Fritch his word that wouldn't happen.

"According to Brogan's story he is able to deal with these underworld characters because they respect him as being a man of his word. If he says he'll do something, he does it. They know that he's on the side of law and order and against blackmail, but they also know that if he gives them his word, his word is as good as his bond."

Drake grinned through cigarette smoke. "Ain't that a hell of a line, Perry?"

"Damned if it isn't," Mason admitted.

"So I suppose Brogan has promised that he can settle for just about half-price, and if the family deals through him they can rest assured there won't be any repetition of the blackmail."

"Something like that. I haven't heard all the line yet," Mason said. "I'm going over and talk with Brogan personally."

"He won't like the idea of you entering the case," Drake warned.

"I know it."

"He'll pretend that he welcomes you with open arms, but if he has a chance he'll stick a knife in your back when you aren't looking."

"I'll be looking," Mason said. "And, in the meantime, if I get a chance to sabotage his little game I'm going to do it."

Drake nodded, then, after a moment, said, "You won't have a chance."

"Why not?"

"Because Brogan is cautious, and Brogan knows your reputation. He respects your ability and he won't take any chances."

"If I can get my hands on that tape recording," Mason said, "I wouldn't have the slightest compunction about destroying it."

"Sure not," Drake agreed, "but you won't get the chance. You're underestimating Brogan."

"Perhaps I am," Mason admitted.

"I tell you the guy's clever. They haven't been able to pin anything on him. He still gets by. He does right well for himself. He has plenty of this world's goods."

"Okay," Mason said. "You get your men on the job. I want to know what happens after I have left Brogan."

"Why is he having the interview in his apartment instead of at his office?" Drake asked.

"I don't know," Mason said. "It may be he doesn't trust some of the help in his office."

"He doesn't trust anyone," Drake said, "but he has some reason—he's pulled plenty of deals in his office."

Mason shrugged. "Anyway, this one's to be at his apartment."

"How long will you be there?"

"Probably about an hour."

"Well," Drake said, "that will give me time to get my operatives spotted. Don't worry, Perry, I'll have the place covered."

"Okay," Mason said, "I'm leaving it up to you."

One of the telephones rang. Drake picked up the receiver, said, "Hello," then said into the instrument, "Just a minute. I have a rush job for you. You know George Brogan. I want him tailed."

He cupped his hand over the mouthpiece, said, "All right, Perry, I'm getting my men started."

Mason arose from the uncushioned chair, "Okay, Paul, I'm leaving it up to you."

Drake was talking in a low voice into the telephone as Mason left the office.

CHAPTER 3

Promptly on time Perry Mason and his client emerged from the elevator at the floor on which Brogan had his apartment.

Mason's ring was answered almost immediately by a man whose figure had all the aesthetic grace of a spider. He was somewhere in his forties, with a short body, long arms and legs, a thick neck and a bald head on which had been placed a toupee, the hair of which was several shades darker than that on the sides of the head.

"Hello, Mr. Mason," Brogan said, grinning broadly, surveying Mason from large, protruding eyes that seemed to have been slightly bleached.

He grabbed Mason's hand, pumped it up and down in the warmth of an overly enthusiastic greeting.

"I'm certainly glad to meet you! I've heard a lot about you. I've followed your cases with great interest, Mr. Mason, in fact with the greatest admiration. I certainly am enjoying this meeting and hope I can be of some small service to you and to Mr. Bain. And how are you this morning, Mrs. Atwood? It's a real pleasure. Won't you step right in?"

Brogan ushered them into the living room of a sumptuously furnished apartment, closed the door, turned a knurled knob which slid a bolt into place, and then in addition snapped a chain into a socket, a chain that prevented the door from being opened more than an inch or two.

"Have to take precautions," he burbled. "You know how these things go, Mr. Mason. It's rather a tricky matter. I wouldn't want to have a lot of detectives break in on us. Now you understand my position in the matter, Mr. Mason."

"I'm not certain I do," Mason said. "In fact I'm quite certain I don't."

"Well, sit down. Make yourself comfortable. I wanted to have this little session in my apartment rather than in my office because a person never knows just what can happen in an office. One is always subject to interruptions and there's not really the privacy there that one has in his own apartment." He suddenly noted the lawyer's hearing aid and automatically raised his voice.

"Now I'm going to be perfectly frank with you, Mr. Mason. I'm keeping this roll of tape in a safe-deposit box. I have to take elaborate precautions in order to safeguard it. For instance, whenever I have it with me I'm always armed."

Brogan threw back his coat, displayed a shoulder holster in which a gun reposed under his armpit.

"You know how those things are, Mr. Mason."

Brogan chuckled.

"I see how they are now," Mason said.

"Ha ha ha," Brogan laughed. "You do have your little joke, don't you?—Well, Mr. Mason, I'm acting here somewhat in the nature of an intermediary. I happen to have the confidence of Mr. J.J. Fritch, that is, I have placed him in such a position that he has had to give me his confidence."

Brogan nodded and grinned.

"That puts you in rather an unusual position, doesn't it?" Mason asked.

"Oh, I'm always in an unusual position," Brogan said. "I don't mind that. People are always trying to misunderstand me, but I'm very much the same way you are, Mason. I protect my clients. That's my creed. Once I've done that I don't care a snap of my fingers about the rules of the game, the conventional rules that is. I'm here to protect my client."

Mason nodded.

"And that's what I'm going to do."

"Just who is your client?" Mason asked.

"Why," Brogan said, "you are."

"I wasn't aware of it."

"Well, you're acting for Mrs. Atwood, and I consider that I'm acting for Mrs. Atwood, that is, I want the privilege of acting for her, and I may say to both of you that I would consider it a privilege."

"And just what is it you expect to do?" Mason asked.

"I want to do whatever you folks think should be done. There is only one thing that I must insist on, Mr. Mason. In my profession I deal with all sorts and classes of people. Sometimes I deal with ethical people, sometimes I deal with crooks, but I always keep faith. My word is my bond. Now I have assured J.J. that nothing is going to happen to that recording, that it won't leave my possession except on terms that are satisfactory to him.

"Of course, you understand it took quite a bit of manipulating in order to get Fritch to let me have the custody of the only thing he has in the world by way of evidence. Naturally he didn't want to let the recording out of his possession, but I persuaded him that he certainly couldn't get anyone to put up money for him unless he was willing to play fair in return."

"That's the original and there aren't any copies?" Mason asked.

Brogan's eyes grew solemn. "I feel that I can assure you of that."

"What is the ground of your assurance?"

"Well, now, Mr. Mason, you may have to say that it's predicated on a long experience in such matters and on dealing with various types of people. But I feel completely certain that this is all the evidence that exists in the world."

"And what is the position of J.J. Fritch? By the way, is he your client?"

"Mr. Mason, I want to assure you that I am not going to take one cent of compensation from Fritch. Neither am I going to represent him. I am interested in this matter only to the extent that I can protect the interests of innocent people. As far as Mr. Fritch is concerned I do not approve of his methods. I wouldn't represent him. I wouldn't touch him with a ten foot pole. I think the man is resorting to tactics that are closely akin to blackmail, Mr. Mason.

"I am willing to act as intermediary. I am willing to represent Mrs. Atwood in securing possession of certain evidence which she feels, or which she should feel, might be very embarrassing to her family. I certainly am not going to identify myself in any way with that man Fritch. I don't like him. I don't like his tactics. I would certainly never permit my professional reputation to be smirched by engaging in any such nefarious activity."

Mason said, "Suppose we buy this tape recording. Would that be the equivalent of suppressing evidence in a criminal case?"

The smile faded from Brogan's face. His pale eyes studied the lawyer carefully. Then he said, "Goodness, Mr. Mason, that idea has never occurred to me."

"Perhaps it should," Mason said.

"Well, of course," Brogan said, "I'm not a lawyer. I'm only an investigator. In this case I'm only being asked to act as an intermediary. I will only continue to act as an intermediary if I am employed by Mrs. Atwood or by someone in the Bain family. If they employ me to carry on negotiations with Mr. Fritch, I will do my best.

"Now that an attorney has entered the case, Mr. Mason, perhaps *you'd* better be the one to decide on the legality of the transaction.

"Of course, you know and I know that it sounds very bad to talk about suppressing evidence, but on the other hand you know and I know that it is no crime to destroy a forgery.

"Now I am firmly convinced in my own mind, Mr. Mason, that Fritch doesn't have a leg to stand on. I think this recording is a complete forgery, but I'm afraid, Mr. Mason, that it's such a clever forgery it would convince a court or a jury. I hope it wouldn't. But it might, you can't tell.

"Now, of course, Mr. Fritch isn't putting it up to us on a basis of destroying evidence. He's simply asking that Mr. Bain or Mrs. Atwood, if she doesn't want to go to her father, loan Fritch sufficient money so that he can have the means of defending himself against a charge which he claims is completely erroneous."

"The charge has been outlawed under the statute of limitations, hasn't it?"

"I believe it has, Mr. Mason, but there again I'm not an attorney. The point is that Mr. Fritch feels he is being falsely accused, that as a good friend Mr. Bain should advance him sufficient money to see that he is capable of carrying on an investigation and a defense."

"Who would make that investigation?" Mason asked. "Would you?"

"Mr. Mason, I'm sure I don't know. You keep insisting on getting the cart before the horse. Of course, it is possible that Mr. Fritch might retain me to make an investigation for him. I don't know. If he retained me *after* this matter had been completely terminated I might accept the employment. I really can't say at this time. But I do know this. I wouldn't even discuss the matter with him until this transaction is entirely cleared up."

"How much money does Fritch want?"

"Just enough to carry on his investigation and to clear himself on a charge that he insists is false."

"And does he have some idea of what that would be?"

"Well, of course, it means running down a lot of old trails, Mr. Mason, and digging into a lot of musty records. It's not going to be an easy matter. Fritch feels that the minimum, the very minimum, would be twenty-five thousand dollars."

"That," Mason said, "is a *lot* of money."

"Well, Fritch doesn't consider it in terms of money. He considers it in terms of service, of what it would cost him to defend himself against a false accusation."

"That seems to be rather high," Mason said.

"Well, of course, it may be. You know more about those things than I do. If Mrs. Atwood retains me to present the matter to Mr. Fritch, I certainly will do everything I can to get him to accept the smallest amount possible."

"And what happens after the amount is paid?"

"Well, of course, Mr. Mason, I don't know. I frankly haven't gone into that matter with Fritch. Fritch came to me. I told him that I wouldn't work for *him* under any consideration, but that I would get in touch with Mrs. Atwood, and if she wanted to employ me I would be glad to accept the employment. However, I warned Fritch that in case I accepted employment from Mrs. Atwood my activities would be wholeheartedly devoted to her, and that if I thought this tape recording was a complete falsification I would endeavor to prove that it was."

"And what did Fritch say to that?"

"He said that I could take the tape recording on my professional assurance that nothing would happen to it, and take any steps I wanted to prove that it was genuine. Now I think I've made my position plain."

"Very plain," Mason said dryly. "Now let's hear the tape recording."

Brogan regarded Mason for a moment with an appraisal that was silently hostile.

"Go ahead," Mason said, "let's hear what you have."

"I think we'd better understand each other first, Mr. Mason," Brogan said. "We're not going to get anywhere by trying to question one another's motives. You're an attorney. I assume you have received a retainer from Mrs. Atwood. Now before I take one step in this matter, one single step, I am going to insist that Mrs. Atwood give me a retainer to act on her behalf, and that you, as her attorney, approve of that retainer. Do I make myself plain?"

"In other words, you're going to protect yourself," Mason said.

"You're damn right I am," Brogan said.

"All right," Mason told him. "Let's hear the recording. I take it you're authorized to go that far."

"That far and no further."

"All right, let's listen to it."

Brogan set up a tape recorder, plugged it into a wall socket, went over to the wall, swung back a section of what seemed to be solid wall disclosing a wall safe. He spun the combination on this safe and took out a spool of tape.

"Now, Mr. Mason, as I told you, I have my own professional reputation at stake. I have assured Mr. Fritch that nothing is going to happen to this recording while it is in my hands and that nobody is going to touch it. I'm going to ask you to stay on that side of the table. I want you and Mrs. Atwood to keep entirely away from this machine. I don't want you to try to touch this tape or to inspect it in any way. Now is that understood?"

"You're making the conditions," Mason said.

"I shall expect you to abide by them."

"Any time we don't want to abide by them," Mason said, "we're quite free to walk out."

"You are indeed."

An embroidered silk throw was over the table. Brogan placed the spool of tape on this silk throw beside the transcribing machine. He saw that the controls were adjusted, then put the spool on the machine, and fed the tape through the recording head on to the empty spool.

"Of course," Mason said, smiling, "I wouldn't want to question a man's hospitality, but I for one certainly could use a drink."

"Excuse me, excuse me," Brogan said. "I was so intent on what I was doing I was entirely neglectful of my duties as a host. What would *you* like, Mrs. Atwood?"

"A Scotch and soda," she said.

"I'll have some whisky and water," Mason said, "and if you don't mind I'd like to mix my own."

"Quite all right, quite all right," Brogan said, and his grin disclosed a mouthful of big teeth. "I can appreciate your position, counselor. You have to be suspicious. Now you'll pardon me if I am just as suspicious as you are. You said you wanted to mix your own and I'll take you at your word. If you'll just precede me into the kitchen, Mr. Mason, and if you and Mrs. Atwood will stay in the kitchenette while I'm there we won't have any trouble. In other words, Mr. Mason, I wouldn't want you to use the subterfuge of having me go out to get a drink to create an opportunity to tamper with this tape. Now the kitchen is right through that door and if you and Mrs. Atwood will precede me, please."

Mason and Mrs. Atwood moved dutifully toward the door indicated.

"Some day," Brogan said, "I'm going to get one of these portable bars that manufacture ice that you can keep in the living room, but in the meantime all of my ice is in the refrigerator and the refrigerator is in the kitchen. I hope you understand, Mr. Mason."

"I understand."

"No hard feelings?"

"No hard feelings," Mason said.

In the kitchen Brogan produced glasses. He opened the refrigerator, took out a tray of ice cubes, pressed a lever and the ice cubes popped out into a dish. He stepped toward a butler's pantry and opened a door, disclosing a closet the back of which was lined with shelves that were filled with various bottles.

"Quite an assortment," Mason said.

"It is, indeed, counselor. I make much of my income by buying bankrupt stocks. I had a chance to buy up a bankrupt restaurant a few months ago. I turned the deal to my financial advantage. In fact, the entire wine cellar was left in my hands after a resale of the fixtures. The sale of fixtures got me even on the deal.

"I could, of course, have sold the liquor and made a sweet profit on the transaction, but then I'd have had to pay income tax. As it is the transaction just balances on a cash basis, leaving me with the contents of the wine cellar, which, of course, I am carrying on my books at a most nominal value."

And George Brogan, not only pleased with himself, but pleased at having such an opportune moment to impress Mason with his business shrewdness as well as the legitimate nature of his business activities, rubbed his hands together.

"Help yourself," Brogan invited. "Pour your drinks the way you like them. I appreciate your suspicions, Mr. Mason, and the way you take precautions. I'm taking the same precautions. Each one pours his own drink. Each one puts in his own mixer. Each one drinks from his own glass without putting it down. I'd hate to have you slip a knockout drop in my glass, Mr. Mason, and I'd hate to have you think that I'd slip one in yours."

They put ice cubes in the glasses, poured drinks. Mason went over to the sink and let water from the faucet dribble in on top of the whisky and ice.

"Here's mud in your eye," Brogan said.

"Confusion to our enemies," Mason corrected as he raised the glass to his lips.

Brogan sputtered into dry, cackling laughter. "You're a card, Mr. Mason, you really are, but it's just what I expected. Now shall we go into the other room and listen to the recording?"

Mason stepped hurriedly toward the door.

"Just a moment, just a moment," Brogan said, his voice suddenly cracking like a whip. "I think you don't give me proper respect, Mr. Mason. *I'll* leave the room first. You're not to be in the room with that recording machine unless I'm there—not even for an instant. Do you understand?"

"Oh, pardon me," Mason said. "As a matter of fact I'll have a little more water in my drink anyway."

He stepped back toward the sink.

Brogan stalked into the living room, followed by Mrs. Atwood.

Over the drainboard on the sink was a magnetic knife holder. It was some three inches wide and eight inches long. Eight or nine knives were fastened to it, held in place by magnetic attraction.

Mason pulled off all of these knives. He put his fingers under the flat magnet, raised it from its position and put it in his hip pocket. Then he hurried into the living room, arriving but a few steps behind Mrs. Atwood.

"Now if you'll just stay on that side of the table," Brogan warned, "I'll stay over here. That way there won't be any temptation on your part to do anything that might cause trouble, Mr. Mason. You understand I'm for you one hundred per cent, but I'm forced to protect my own professional reputation for fair dealing."

"Quite commendable. You understand my attitude and I understand yours," Mason said. "If I can wreck Fritch's scheme I'm going to do so."

He placed his glass on the table, drew up a chair, seated himself, and as he did so, surreptitiously slipped the flat magnet out of his hip pocket and under the cloth on the table.

He picked up his glass, took a sip from it, put it down so it was behind the flat magnet. By manipulating his glass slowly from side to side he moved the magnet a few inches toward the recording machine.

"Go right ahead. We're ready any time you are," Mason said.

Brogan flicked a switch, then settled back to watch Mason and Sylvia Atwood.

The recorder gave a few preliminary squawks, then voices that were startlingly clear and distinct filled the room. For fifteen minutes Mason and Sylvia Atwood listened to what purported to be a conversation between J.J. Fritch and Ned Bain relating to the original partnership which had been founded by the men. From that recorded conversation there could be no question but what Ned Bain knew definitely and positively that the money which had been advanced by Fritch was money that had been derived from the robbery of the bank.

"Well," Brogan said, unable to keep a note of triumph from his voice when he had finished the recording, "are you satisfied?"

"Satisfied with what?" Mason asked.

Brogan caught himself quickly. "Satisfied that it is your father's voice?" he asked Mrs. Atwood. "Because if it isn't, that's all there is to it. We'll go right ahead and have Fritch arrested for attempted extortion."

"And if it *is* her father's voice?" Mason asked.

"Then, of course, we're going to have to be more careful."

Mason stood up, his hand resting on the table. He slowly leaned toward the machine, looking down at the recorded tape, pushing the flat magnet ahead of his fingers as his hand slid forward over the cloth.

"Now just a moment, Mr. Mason, just a moment," Brogan said, suddenly wary. "That's far enough."

Mason said, "I want to look at that spool. I want to see whether it's been spliced."

His finger tips pushed the magnet under the cloth.

"Spliced?" Brogan asked. "What difference would that make?"

"It might make a lot."

"Well, it hasn't been spliced. I can assure you of that, although I still don't see what you're getting at."

Brogan rewound the tape back on its proper spool, lifted it off the machine.

Mason abruptly leaned forward, giving the magnet a last push as he did so.

"Let me look at that spool, Brogan," he said.

Brogan put the spool on the table, said, "Mason, don't try anything. I'm going to have to ask you to step back, then I'll show you the whole spool."

"Certainly," Mason said, stepping well back out of the way. "I want to see if it's been spliced."

Brogan said, "After all, this is a business matter with both of us. You're representing a client. I'm hoping to represent that same client. Our interests are in common. You've been through deals of this sort before and so have I. Now let's keep our heads and discuss the matter on a logical, adult basis."

Brogan put a lead pencil down through the center of the spool and unwound some fifteen feet of tape, letting it fall on the floor.

"Now, you see," he said, "there isn't a splice in it."

"Not in that much of it," Mason said.

Brogan reeled off another ten or fifteen feet, then with the forefinger of his other hand wound the tape back onto the spool, revolving the spool on the pencil while it was flat on the table.

"Well, that's all that you're going to see right now," he said. "I haven't permission to go any further. I can assure you that tape isn't spliced. So far as I know there's nothing whatever wrong with it. It's absolutely genuine and authentic."

Brogan picked up the spool, said, "Now I'm going to put this spool back in the safe before we do any more talking."

Brogan momentarily turned his back to put the spool in the safe. Mason, leaning forward, ostensibly to inspect the recording machine, slipped the magnet out from under the cloth.

Sylvia Atwood's green eyes suddenly widened as she saw Mason putting something in his hip pocket. Mason motioned her to silence.

"Well," Mason said, "I'll help myself to another drink if you don't mind, Brogan, and then we'll sit down and talk business."

He stepped out in the kitchen, swiftly put the magnetic knife holder back into place, put the knives in their proper place, and was pouring more whisky into his glass when Brogan and Mrs. Atwood appeared in the doorway.

"Help yourself," Brogan said, "I'm sorry if I was a little suspicious, Mason, but frankly, I'm just a little afraid of you. You have a reputation for being damnably clever that I thoroughly respect."

Mason said, "All right, let's get down to brass tacks. Fritch *wants* twenty-five thousand dollars. How much will he *take?*"

"I think twenty," Brogan said, his eyes narrowing. "I think if I were representing Mrs. Atwood I could save her a cool five thousand dollars."

"What would be your terms?"

"Terms!" Brogan said. "Why, Mr. Mason, I'd simply want a reasonable compensation. I'd leave that matter entirely in your hands, absolutely in your hands as an attorney who's experienced in these matters and who can appreciate the gravity of the situation and knows what this record could well be worth."

Mason sipped his drink thoughtfully. "Look here, Brogan, I'm not going to advise my client to pay a cent, or to employ you to act as intermediary in paying a red cent until I'm certain that tape is a genuine recording. Now you don't want me to put my hands on it. I tell you what we'll do. Play the tape once more, but let me sit where I can watch it while it goes through the recording head so I can see there aren't any splices in it."

"Why all the bother about splices?" Brogan asked. "What difference would a splice make?"

"Simply this, there might be parts of two conversations on there, so blended and scrambled that Mr. Bain's answers might have been to some other question altogether."

Brogan threw back his head and laughed. "That's such a far-fetched idea, Mason. I doubt that it could even be done."

"I know damn well it could be done," Mason said.

"Well, I'm certain it *wasn't* done."

"I don't care about how you feel. *I* want to be certain."

"How? What can I do to assure you?"

"I want you to run that tape again while I'm sitting beside you."

Brogan shook his head. "I couldn't permit that."

"Well," Mason said, "I've got to see the inside of that tape. I've got to see that it isn't spliced."

"I'll tell you what I'll do," Brogan said. "I'll turn the machine around. In that way you can remain on your side of the table yet watch the tape as it unwinds."

"That'll be satisfactory," Mason said. "I want to hear it once more anyway."

"Why do you want to hear it again?"

"Frankly, because I want to become familiar with Ned Bain's voice."

"It's his voice all right."

"I'm sorry I can't accept your assurance."

"I wouldn't ask you to. I'm just telling you. I might save you some work."

"Oh, I don't mind work."

Brogan led the way back to the living room, switched on the tape recording machine, then went once more to the wall safe and twisted the dials, standing slightly to one side so that he could watch Mason as he did so.

Brogan removed the spool of tape, placed it on the machine, fed it through the recording head, turned the machine around so that Mason could see the inside of the tape, and stepped back, his arms folded, his eyes watchful.

The machine made a few preliminary noises. The tape slowly unwound. There was complete silence.

"Well," Mason said, "what's the matter? Start it playing. You haven't put it in wrong, have you?"

Sudden panic seized Brogan. He leaned forward and adjusted the controls of the machine.

"Be certain you aren't erasing that tape as you're feeding it through," Mason warned.

Brogan abruptly shut off the machine, studied the connections carefully, then again threaded the tape through.

"No chance of that," he said. "I've played thousands of tapes on this machine. I know what I'm doing. Keep back, Mason."

"I'm back," Mason said. "I thought perhaps I might help you."

"I can get along without your help."

Once more Brogan started the tape winding through the recording head.

Again there was a period of complete silence. After a long interval a faint sound of a few words emanated in a conversation that was inaudible.

Brogan turned up the volume to its maximum capacity.

The tape continued to unwind. Occasionally it was possible to hear a very faint word, but not distinctly enough to tell what was being said.

"Good God!" Brogan said under his breath. Beads of perspiration appeared on his forehead. He suddenly looked up at Mason, his eyes suspicious. "What did you do to this machine?" he shouted.

"What *could* I have done to it?" Mason asked.

"I'm damned if I know," Brogan said. He switched the machine off, rewound the tape by hand. "I think you've reversed the magnets in some way. It hasn't done you a damn bit of good, Mason. I'll get another machine. I'll—"

"Do so by all means," Mason told him. "And when you do, and get that playing again to your satisfaction, would you mind calling me? Before I advise Mrs. Atwood to retain you to enter into negotiations with Mr. Fritch, I want to assure myself that that's a genuine tape recording."

Brogan controlled himself by an effort. He wiped perspiration from his forehead. "You don't need to worry about its being genuine."

"It seems to worry you that it might *not* be genuine."

"I have my professional reputation to consider. If anything's happened to that tape I'd be in a tight spot."

"So you've told us a good many times. Well, I can count on you to give me a ring when you've got another tape recorder set up and have the spool ready to put in operation?"

"You can indeed," Brogan said, righting to keep a semblance of composure. "I'm quite satisfied it'll be all right, Mr. Mason."

"That's fine," Mason told him. "We'll be back."

"It's something wrong with the machine," Brogan said. "It has to be with the machine. The magnets have become polarized or something. I'll get another machine up here, probably some time tomorrow."

"That's fine," Mason said. "Give me a ring and we'll make an appointment. I'm fairly busy in court right at the moment."

Brogan escorted them to the door, took off the safety chain, spun back the knurled knob, opened the door and said, "Well, thank you very much for coming in. It's about lunch-time. Sorry that I can't ask you to have lunch with me, but I'm going to be busy trying to get that machine adjusted, trying to find out just what the devil happened to it."

His pale eyes stared at Mason. "Just what the devil *did* happen to it?" he asked. "I don't think it'll make much difference on the tape recording, Mr. Mason, but it was a damn fine trick. Personally I'd like to know what the trick was."

"Trick?" Mason asked.

"You said it," Brogan said, hesitated a moment, and then slammed the door.

Standing there in the hallway, they heard the chain snap into place, heard the bolt rasp into its socket.

"Well," Mason said to Sylvia Atwood, "that's that."

"Mr. Mason," she whispered, "what *did* you do? What was that you put in your pocket? What was it that was under the silk cover on that table?"

Mason looked at her innocently. "I wouldn't know."

Abruptly she smiled. "No, I'm quite sure you wouldn't."

"Well," Mason told her, "I'll get in touch with you when I hear from Brogan again."

"You think you'll hear from him soon?"

"Oh, certainly," Mason told her. "He'll have some things to do first, a good story to think up, and then he'll be his affable self once more. He'll assure us there was only a minor defect in the playback mechanism. He'll have it all fixed by tomorrow."

"Mr. Mason, what in the world *did* you do? It sounded as though you'd managed to erase every bit of conversation on that tape!"

Mason raised his eyebrows in surprise. "*I* did?"

"Yes."

"How in the world could I have done that with Brogan watching me all the time?"

She led the way toward the elevator. "I presume that question is worrying Mr. George Brogan at the present time."

Mason grinned. "Particularly in view of his assurance that there was only one recording of that conversation in existence and no dubbed copies."

"And," she went on lightly, "your hearing aid seems to have a lot to do with your success in these matters. Do you wear it often?"

"I have a slight cold," Mason told her, and opening the elevator door, stood to one side for her to enter.

CHAPTER 4

Mason's private office looked as if it could well have been the laboratory in some sound studio.

Mason's miniature wire recorder was on the desk. A connection led from it to a tape recorder which was so arranged that a recording could be made on tape directly from the miniature wire recorder. In addition to that, a monitoring attachment enabled Mason and Della Street to hear what was being recorded.

"That certainly comes in good and clear," Della Street said.

Mason nodded.

"What about Brogan?"

"He's going to have to show his hand," Mason said. "He'll rush out to see Fritch. When that happens Drake's men will be on the job. He—"

Mason broke off as a code knock sounded on the door of his private office.

"That's Paul now, Della."

Della Street opened the door.

Paul Drake, good humored in his gangling, double-jointed way, entered the room, pushed the door shut behind him, grinned and said, "What the deuce are you folks doing in here?"

Mason grinned. "I used my little German wire recorder to record the conversation with your friend Brogan, and incidentally, to make my own copy of the tape recording that he had."

Drake listened. "Seems to come in clear enough. What are you doing with that tape machine?"

"Transferring from wire to tape," Mason explained. "I'll use the tape for reference and lock the wire away as original evidence."

Drake continued to listen, then chuckled, "You seem to have Brogan going. Is this after the recording was played?"

"That's right. I asked him to play it the second time. What's happened with Brogan? Has he led your men to J.J. Fritch yet?"

"Not yet. He hasn't even gone out."

Mason's voice showed his surprise. "You mean he hasn't left his apartment?"

"No. My men are stationed there."

"How long have they—"

"Plenty of time. They were there before you and Mrs. Atwood left. They saw you going out."

Mason frowned, then let a smile erase the frown. "That means Brogan is having one hell of a time trying to find out what happened to his tape recording. He doesn't dare to report to Fritch."

"Gosh, Perry, what actually *did* happen?"

Mason grinned. "I messed up Brogan's evidence."

"How?"

"To be perfectly frank with you," Mason said, "it was an idea that came to me on the spur of the moment. I thought I might ask for a drink and perhaps get him out of the room so I could at least look at the tape and see if it had been spliced. He was too smart for that."

"He would be," Drake said. "Gosh, Perry, the way that guy plays the game he wouldn't have left you alone with that tape recording for a minute. According to his code of ethics it would have been all right for you to have grabbed the tape and thrown it out of the window."

"I know," Mason said. "He insisted on all three of us going into the kitchen. Then he was so afraid I'd put knockout drops in his drink, or that I would think that he might have drugged ours that he insisted on everyone mixing his own drink. I noticed a magnetic knife holder over the drain-board and that was when I got a sudden idea."

"What did you do?"

"Managed to be the last one to leave the kitchen, pulled the knives off the magnetic holder, slipped the holder out of its socket, and had a nice flat magnet which I was able to insert under the cloth on the table just where I felt certain he was going to put the spool of tape. He didn't notice there was anything under the cloth. I raised the point that I wanted to see some of the tape, so he obligingly rotated the spool while it was within the magnetic field and, of course, erased everything on it."

"Did what?" Drake asked incredulously.

"Erased everything on it."

"I don't get it," Drake said. "How did it erase?"

Mason grinned. "A tape recorder is simply an arrangement of molecules on a magnetized tape. You can erase the conversation and use the tape over and over again by bringing it through a magnetic field, which is, roughly speaking, what happens when you use the tape a second time. As it goes through a magnetic field the old conversation is erased just before the new conversation is put on.

"You can take a good horseshoe magnet, run it around a spool of tape and erase everything on it, but a good flat magnet works a lot better."

"Well I'll be darned," Drake said. "I never knew that. That is, I never thought of it in exactly that way. I knew, of course, that conversations were recorded due to pulsations in a magnetic field. What did Brogan do? I'll bet he had a fit."

Mason chuckled. "He certainly was in a panic for a minute. Then he probably remembered that he had means of duplicating the tape, so he rushed us out of there, assuring us it was something wrong with the machine."

"Does he know what you did?"

"He knows I messed it up some way," Mason said, "but he doesn't know how, and that's worrying him a lot."

"But if he's lost that tape recording then what?"

"That tape recording," Mason said, "was synthetic."

"What do you mean?"

"I mean this—Fritch probably got Ned Bain into a long conversation about a lot of things, politics, old times, business, cattle, oil and all the rest of it. Then Fritch went to some sound recording studio. He ran off portions of the tape recording of his conversation with Ned Bain, and some unscrupulous sound technician helped him fix up a master roll of spliced conversation."

"I still don't get it."

"Just this way, Paul. Let's suppose that in their actual conversation Fritch said to Bain, 'You remember that time we killed the big deer up by the point of the mountain?' and Bain said, 'I remember it just as plain as day, J.J. I never will forget it.'

"All right, Fritch goes to a sound studio. They take that answer that Bain made and on another tape Fritch says, 'You remember the time I raised capital for your oil well venture in Texas by holding up that bank, Ned?'

"Then the sound technician cuts out that part of the tape-recorded conversation where Ned Bain says, 'I remember it just as plain as day, J.J. I never will forget it,' and splices that right in so that it seems an answer to Fritch's question."

Drake said, "You mean the whole conversation was put together that way?"

"That's right."

"Then the tape is a mass of splices?"

"The original tape must be," Mason said, "but the splices have been cunningly made. They're handled in such a way that you can't possibly detect them by listening. Then that master tape was boiled down to about twenty minutes of generalized conversation with four or five very incriminating statements incorporated in it. After that was done the whole thing was dubbed on another spool of tape, which is supposed to be the original sound recording of a conversation."

"How are you going to prove all that?" Drake asked.

"That, of course," Mason admitted, "is the problem. I think I have a clue and a good one."

"What's that?"

"The sound technician was too clever."

"What do you mean?"

"The actual conversation between Fritch and Bain took place in a room or in an apartment somewhere. The voices bounced back from the walls. You can hear just the faint sound of an echo whenever Ned Bain is talking. You hear it sometimes when Fritch is talking. But whenever Fritch asks a question to which Ned Bain makes an incriminating answer, Fritch's question comes in without the faintest sound of echo.

"You can see what that means. That question was asked in a soundproof room in a studio somewhere, and while Fritch tried his best, probably with careful coaching, to make it sound like a casual question as part of the other conversation, the fine quality of the recording during those particular periods is manifest even to an untrained ear.

"You see, what happens in an ordinary room, Paul, is that a voice, particularly if it's a man's heavy voice, bounces back in a whole series of echoes, from the floor, the walls and the ceiling. In ordinary conversation we focus those sounds out and the ear doesn't hear them, but when you record the conversation through a sensitive microphone, every one of those echoes is picked up.

"Sound studios naturally can't afford to have that happen, so they use soundproof rooms with specially prepared walls that break up the echoes so there isn't any voice bounce.

"Now I've listened pretty carefully to that tape recording and at no time do I find Ned Bain making any actual admission. All that Ned Bain does is to make statements confirming certain things J.J. Fritch has said. I think for that reason we can prove the tape recording is a fake if we have to, but the method I used today is going to prove it, provided we get a break."

"What do you think happened?"

"I think that just about as soon as we got out of there Brogan phoned Fritch and said, 'Mason managed to do something to erase the conversation on this spool we have. We'll have to make another

copy from the master record. Then we'll destroy this tape recording and substitute the new one. I'll tell Mason it was a defect in the
machine. Mason will know I'm lying, but there's nothing he can do
about it. There's nothing he can prove.' Then Fritch and Brogan will
run off another dubbed copy and tell me that's the same one I listened
to, that the trouble wasn't with the tape but with the playback."

Drake thought that over. "Can you prove that the substitute is a
new recording, Perry?"

"No."

"Then what did you gain by erasing that first recording?"

"It's going to force Brogan to get in touch with Fritch. When he
does that we'll have a line on Fritch. It's also going to force them to
make another copy of that master recording. They've got that master spool of spliced tape locked away somewhere in a safe-deposit
box. By following Brogan to Fritch and Fritch to the bank we'll
know where the master spool is located. Then we'll slap a *subpoena
duces tecum* on Fritch ordering him to produce the spool of spliced
tape from box number so-and-so in the safe-deposit vault at such-
and-such a bank. It will scare them to death. They won't know how
much we know."

"But Brogan hasn't left his apartment."

"Probably because Fritch is out some place and he's been unable
to get in touch with him."

"What about your client? Does she know you sabotaged the
tape?"

"She knows it, but she doesn't know how I did it. Brogan knows
and it's frightened him. He'd give a good deal to know how it was
done."

"Well, my men are on the job," Drake said. "I thought I'd check
with you."

Mason nodded.

"You think you can hear the difference in quality of conversation when Fritch asks one of those incriminating questions?"

"I think," Mason said, "that even this little recorder I have did
a good enough job of reproducing so you can hear it on the copy.

Of course, you must remember that it was coming in over a loud-speaker and there was a certain amount of echo from the walls and ceiling of Brogan's apartment. However, those voice bounces would be equally distributed over all the conversation so that there'll still be a better quality of recording in the incriminating questions asked by Fritch."

Mason threw a switch on the tape recorder, shut off the wire recorder, spun the tape recorder back for a few minutes, then turned it on to the playback and let Drake listen.

"Now this part of the conversation," Mason said, "is coming in just about equally clear, as Fritch's voice and Bain's voice have about the same number of echoes. They're talking about the cattle business there. Now listen to this."

Suddenly Fritch's voice said, "I'm wondering what will happen if anyone should ever find out that I'm the one who committed the bank robbery." And Bain answered casually, so casually in fact that he seemed to be discussing some routine matter, "How are they ever going to find out, J.J.?"

Mason cut off the machine. "See what I mean, Paul?"

"I'm not certain that I do," Drake said. "I heard Fritch's question very plainly. The thing that impressed me was the fact that Bain took it all so casually."

"He took it casually," Mason said, "because he was talking about something else. I'm going to play it once more. Now you listen. Even in this dubbed copy you can hear the difference in quality if you listen closely. Fritch asked that question in a studio. Now I'll turn it back and you listen carefully."

Mason turned back the machine. Drake closed his eyes so he could listen to better advantage.

This time when Mason shut off the machine Drake was nodding.

"I get you now, Perry. You can sure hear a difference in quality there."

"Of course," Mason went on, "you can't hear it on this dubbed recording anywhere near as well as you can on the original record."

"If that occurs to them couldn't they fix it up?" Drake asked.

"Sure," Mason admitted. "They'd make a new master tape with Fritch's questions asked in an apartment where there'd be a normal voice bounce. Then they'd make a new copy. But, try as they could, they couldn't get Fritch to ask the same questions, even if they used a script. There'd be a word different here and there, a change of pace or of expression.

"That's the advantage of having this recording. If they change it in the least, or change the wording of Fritch's questions, I'll flash this recording on them and claim that they made two different recordings. That's what I was hoping would happen when I went over there this morning. I was hoping I could get a copy of the recording they had and then frighten them into trying to fake a new recording that would have some different element injected into it. Then I'd be able to prove conclusively that the whole thing was a put-up job."

"That, of course, would be better than relying on the difference in quality on the sound recording," Drake said.

"I'll probably do it yet," Mason told him. "But I couldn't resist the temptation to erase that tape recording right under Brogan's nose."

"It'll give him more respect for you," Drake said. "He—"

Della Street's phone rang. She picked up the receiver and Drake waited to see if the call was for him.

Della Street cupped her hand over the mouthpiece and said, "Mr. Brogan is calling you, Chief."

Mason grinned, said, "I'll take it. Tell Gertie to switch it on to my line."

Mason picked up his telephone and said, "Hello."

Brogan's voice said, "I just wanted you to know that I've located the trouble in the machine."

"Indeed," Mason said, and added dryly, "I trust that the tape wasn't ruined."

"No, no, no, no, nothing like that," Brogan said. "The tape is *quite* all right. There was nothing wrong with the tape at all. It was simply a loose connection in the machine itself that prevented the conversation from being broadcast over the loud-speaker so that you could hear it. The tape is quite all right. The machine is fixed and everything's working perfectly now."

"That's fine," Mason said. "Where are you now? At your apartment?"

"At my apartment?" Brogan said in some surprise. "Heavens, no. I'm at my office."

"Oh, I thought perhaps you were still tinkering with the machine."

"I took the machine to a repair shop," Brogan said. "They found the loose connection."

"Then you haven't played the tape back?"

"No, I haven't played it back, but I have played other tapes so that I know the machine is working."

"And you're not sure then that the defect in the machine didn't erase the other tape?"

"It couldn't have."

"But you haven't played it back?"

"I've played back just an inch or two of it to make sure."

"And it came in all right?"

"Clear as a bell. It's really a very good recording, all things considered."

"Of course," Mason said, "you understand my position, Brogan. I'll have to hear it again to make sure you're not kidding me about the tape."

"I want you to," Brogan said.

"Where, when?"

"As soon as possible. How about tomorrow morning at nine o'clock at my apartment. Will that be too early?"

"No, that's fine," Mason told him. "The early hour suits me. I'll be there."

"Thank you," Brogan said and hung up.

Mason turned to Paul Drake. "Brogan says he's at his office, but he's found the trouble, which was in the loudspeaker attachment on the machine, that everything's all ready to go, that the tape was not hurt in the least, that at nine o'clock tomorrow morning at his apartment he'll give us another playback.

"Now we know he hasn't left his apartment. You know what that means, Paul. It means the master tape is located somewhere in his apartment, that he has a series of machines there just as I have here, and that he's made another dubbing and has completed it. He said he was at his office, yet we know he's still in his apartment."

"That means he has the master recording and Fritch doesn't," Drake said.

Mason nodded. "Apparently so."

"You want me to keep my men on the job?"

"Keep them on the job," Mason instructed. "I want Brogan shadowed, but we now know that he has the master recording."

Mason's telephone shrilled into noise and Della Street, answering, said, "Yes, Gertie, who is it. . . . Just a second, Gertie."

She cupped her hand over the mouthpiece of the telephone, said to Mason, "It's Sylvia Atwood. She says it's terribly important. She simply must speak to you right away."

Mason nodded, picked up the telephone, said, "Hello," and heard Sylvia Atwood's voice, sharp with excitement.

"Mr. Mason, you must come at once. Something terrible has happened."

"What?"

"Fritch telephoned Dad and told him that he had to dismiss you or he would sell his story to the bank. J.J. said he felt there was no call for him to have any further loyalty to Dad, that he was going to play the thing for his own best interests. At first, of course, Dad didn't have the faintest idea of what he was talking about, and then gradually Fritch kept on until it dawned on him. Dad's had a terrible upset. He knows now an attempt is being made to blackmail us on the oil property.

"We thought the very best way possible of reassuring Dad would be to let him talk with you. I think you can reassure him and do more good than all the doctor's medicine in the world."

"You want me to see him?"

"Yes, please."

"When?"

"Just as soon as possible. Right away, if you possibly can."

"You're out there with him now?"

"No. I'm downtown. I could be in your office in five minutes, drive you out and bring you back."

Mason said, "Just a minute." He raised his head, frowned in thoughtful concentration for a moment, then said, "All right, come on in. I'll go out with you."

Mason hung up the telephone, said to Paul Drake, "Now why would Fritch pull a stunt like that?"

"Like what?"

"Ringing up Ned Bain and telling him that he had to dismiss me."

"Well, why not?"

"Because," Mason said, "the best hold Fritch had on the family was on the theory that Ned Bain mustn't know anything at all about what was going on. Now then, Fritch has deliberately thrown that card away. Apparently it was a trump card. Why did he do it?"

"Because he thinks he has something to gain by doing it," Drake said.

"That," Mason told him, "is obvious. Now then, the question is, what did he have to gain?"

Drake shrugged his shoulders.

Mason said to Della, "Sylvia Atwood is going to be here within five minutes. I'm going out to call on her father and do what I can to reassure him.

"In the meantime, Paul, you keep your men covering Brogan. Brogan and Fritch have been in communication, probably by telephone since Brogan hasn't left his apartment. Of course, Fritch *could* have come to Brogan there at the apartment."

"You don't know Fritch?"

Mason shook his head.

"Have we got a description?"

"We could probably get one," Mason said, "but I don't know that it would do any good now. I was thinking that Brogan would go to Fritch and that Fritch must have the master recording. Apparently it's the other way around. Fritch must have gone to Brogan. Brogan must have the master recording."

"That checks," Drake said. "Brogan is the brains behind the blackmail."

"All right," Mason told him, "we'll play it on that basis for a while."

CHAPTER 5

Mason, sitting on Sylvia Atwood's right, noticed approvingly the deft manner with which she handled the car in traffic.

The lawyer sat with arms folded, his keen eyes missing nothing, his face granite hard with expressionless impassivity.

From time to time Sylvia stole a quick sidelong glance at Mason's profile, then devoted her attention to driving.

After they had negotiated the heaviest part of the traffic and were rolling along on a boulevard, she said bitterly, "J.J. has thrown off the mask now and shown himself for what he is—a blackmailer, a dirty, vicious blackmailer."

Mason nodded.

"But," she went on, "how can he do anything to hurt Dad without at the same time hurting himself? He's going to have to admit that he was the one who robbed the bank."

"Was *one* of the persons who robbed the bank," Mason corrected.

"Well," she said, "it doesn't make any difference as far as we're concerned."

"Why?"

"Because it's simply a question of whether Dad knew that he was using stolen money, but it would seem to me that J.J. has completely reversed his position. Before this he was trying to protect himself and his good name. Now he's engaged in blackmail, pure and simple."

"Blackmail," Mason said, "is never pure and it's seldom simple."

"No, I suppose not, but why shouldn't he try to protect himself?"

"Because," Mason said, "they've had some very clever attorneys looking up the statute of limitations, and they've decided that the lapse of time has made Fritch immune from prosecution on any charge. That's probably why the police haven't swooped down on Fritch and arrested him for that bank job. It's up to the bank in a civil suit to try to recover its property—"

"But doesn't a statute of limitations run against a bank?"

"There," Mason said, "you're up against a peculiar, tricky legal situation. In certain types of involuntary trust, where the custodian of the property is presumed to have knowledge of the illegal means by which the property was acquired, and the other person has no knowledge and is prevented from having knowledge by the secretive acts of the involuntary trustee, the statute of limitations may run from the *discovery* of the facts rather than the facts themselves."

"Oh, you lawyers!" she said. "You're *so* technical."

"You have to have technicalities if you're going to have law," Mason said. "The minute you lay down a line of demarcation between right and wrong you are necessarily going to have border-line cases. Go down to the border between Mexico and the United States. Stand two inches on this side of the border and you're in the United States. Stand two inches on the other side and you're in Mexico and subject to the laws of Mexico. That means that moving four inches puts you under an entirely different set of laws."

"Well, that's understandable."

"It's understandable to you," Mason said, "because you can clearly see the boundary line between the United States and Mexico and can understand it. The lawyer sees legal boundary lines just as clearly and can readily comprehend the distinction between being barely on one side of the line and barely on the other.

"Tell me something about your family that we're going to see."

"My father is magnificent. He's been a wonderful, wonderful man. But he's a sick man now."

"And there's a sister?"

"Hattie."

"What about her?"

"She's wonderful, Mr. Mason. Just wait until you meet her. As I told you she's a stay-at-home, but she has the most wonderful disposition.

"When the man who was to be my husband showed up and started courting me, Hattie insisted I should go ahead and marry and she'd stay home and take care of the family."

"Your mother was living then?"

"Yes."

"And you did that?"

"Yes, I did. I suppose I was selfish, but I was in love and—well, I did it, and Hattie stayed on, taking care of the folks, running the house.

"She's wonderful—and now she's having her own chance for happiness."

"Tell me about that," Mason said.

"His name is Edison Levering Doyle. You'll meet him. He's clever. I think he's going places. I feel so happy for Hattie—and yet I'm afraid for her."

"Why are you afraid?" Mason asked.

"It's difficult to describe."

"Can you try?"

"Yes, I can try, but I don't want to."

"Go ahead," Mason said. "What is it?"

"Well, I'm afraid Hattie isn't going to be happy with Edison, and I'm afraid it's going to break her heart, but I don't know what I can do about it."

"That isn't what you started to say," Mason told her.

"All right," she said, "I'll put it right on the line with you, Mr. Mason. Perhaps I never saw it clearly before. Perhaps it's because I've been out traveling and meeting people. Perhaps it's something that a sheltered, circumscribed existence has done to Hattie. I don't know.

"However—oh, I don't know how to tell you—life has a way of doing things to you. You don't realize that the minutes that pass by are shaping your character. You can't—you can't wait things out. Now I'm just making a mess of it. I knew I would."

Mason said, "You mean that Hattie has become somewhat drab, colorless, mousy?"

"I didn't say that."

"That's what you mean?"

"It sounds horrible when you say it that way, Mr. Mason, but—and yet I don't know how to tell you *exactly* what I mean. Let's take two girls. Let's suppose that they're absolutely equal and identical, if you could suppose such a thing. One of them makes herself attractive to men. She likes masculine company. She's on the go. Men make passes at her and she likes it. She wears good clothes, goes to beauty parlors, travels, sees glamorous women, and naturally she has a tendency to become—well, a little glamorous."

"Go on," Mason said.

"Then we'll suppose that the other woman stays home. She doesn't have time to go to a beauty parlor. She doesn't care because no one is going to see her anyway. She does her hair herself. She doesn't go out much to parties. She's constantly waiting on older people. She's constantly associating with them. She—well, after a year or two of that what's going to happen?"

"You mean the stay-at-home girl is going to lose her charm?"

"She isn't going to develop any."

"But you have just told me that Hattie is now going to have her chance with Edison Doyle."

"I *hope* she's going to have her chance, but—well, a man wants a lot of things in a woman. He wants a mate. He wants someone to keep his home. He wants someone to raise his children. He wants a companion. He also wants fun."

"Are you trying to tell me," Mason asked, "that Edison Doyle was happy with Hattie until he began to see more of you, and then lately you felt he was comparing you and Hattie and perhaps becoming a little interested in you?"

"Good heavens, am I *that* obvious?"

"Is that what you're trying to tell me?"

"Well, not exactly, but—Damn it, that's what I was trying *not* to tell you. I don't even know. I can't eve. . . ."

"It worries you?" Mason asked as her voice trailed away into silence.

"In a way."

"Tell me a little more about yourself. You married, and then what? Were you happy?"

"I married Sam Atwood. We were happy. It was a wonderful life. Then Sam died. It was quite a shock. However, I'm a person who adjusts readily to a new environment.

"Sam left me insurance, stocks, bonds, real estate—some good investments. I have made a few good investments of my own. I've been lucky."

"How long ago did your husband die?"

"About eighteen months."

"And what have you been doing since?"

"I've been traveling. I had always wanted to travel. After Sam's death there was no reason why I shouldn't."

"You didn't travel before?"

"Not too much. My husband had business interests that kept him pretty well occupied. He couldn't get too far away from those business interests.

"His death was a shock to me. I wanted to get into a new environment, to meet new people, to see new things. I traveled."

"And you learned something from your travels?"

"I suppose so. I think one does. I've been trying to tell you that I think every day of one's life places a stamp on the individual. You select the sort of life you want to live, and living that life in turn leaves its mark, so that you're changing all the time, one way or the other."

"How long have you been back home?"

"About thirty days."

"You came back and found Edison Doyle and Hattie engaged?"

"Not exactly engaged but going together, and I think there's sort of an understanding. Dad's heart is very bad. I suppose he can't last too long. I think Hattie wants to be with him. Dad has grown to a point where he depends on her."

"And when you came back from your travels you saw Hattie through new eyes?"

"Mr. Mason, I was shocked. I didn't realize—it's so hard to explain, so hard to describe, that I'm not even going to try."

"And Edison Doyle, on the other hand, saw in you a glamorous potential sister-in-law. He started out to be nice to you and now you find him perhaps contrasting you and Hattie?"

"I don't know *what's* happening, Mr. Mason. I like Edison. He's a wonderful guy. I think he's taken life a little too seriously. I think he needs to be jolted out of it. He could marry, settle down and become quite a stick-in-the-mud. On the other hand, he could be jarred out of his shell of seriousness and get a broader outlook."

"What does he do?"

"He's an architect."

"You're around home a good deal?"

"I try to be with Dad some. I'd like to take some of the load off Hattie. I'd like to stay with Dad and have her get out. I think she and Edison should go out more. I think she should pay more attention to her clothes, more attention to her personal appearance."

"How does she feel?"

"It's hard to tell how Hattie feels. Of course, Dad's heart is in such shape that he may pass away at any time. It may be rather sudden. I think Hattie wants to be sure that she's with him, that if he ever should call for her she'd be there."

"And you?"

"I don't see things that way, Mr. Mason. Dad may go tomorrow. He may live for years. I've talked with the doctor about it. No one knows. I have my own problems. I have my own apartment. I have my own friends. I have my own life. I try to keep myself well dressed and attractive. I try to be with Dad some. I've repeatedly put pressure on Hattie to hire nurses so that she could get out."

"She doesn't want that?"

"She doesn't want it, and lately she's been just a little—oh, I don't know, sometimes I think she's—well, we don't see things the same way."

"You think perhaps she feels that her boy-friend is becoming attracted by your glamour and is perhaps a little jealous?"

"Good heavens, Mr. Mason, Hattie wouldn't get jealous. She might get hurt but she wouldn't get jealous."

"Well?" Mason asked.

"Well, Mr. Mason, when I'm with Edison I'm not going to sit around with my hands on my lap and look down at my feet. I accepted Edison as a future brother-in-law. I joked with him and laughed. I like life and laughter and—I think you're prying into things that don't necessarily enter into the case, Mr. Mason, or perhaps I'm telling you things that I shouldn't. This discussion is—well, perhaps you're jumping at conclusions. I think you'd better wait until you've seen things for yourself."

"And what about the rest of the family?" Mason asked. "Tell me about the others."

"Jarrett is an archaeologist. He's always around sticking his nose into ruins somewhere. Right at present he's down in Yucatan."

"And his wife?"

"His wife is filthy rich and terribly snooty."

"In other words, she doesn't like you."

"And I don't like her. However, it's been a good match for Jarrett. Because of her money he's been able to go around digging up ruins, looking at old carvings with a magnifying glass."

"I take it he's more like Hattie than like you?"

"He isn't like anyone except Jarrett Bain. He's a character. He'll sit while you're talking and look at you steadily with gray eyes regarding you through spectacles so thick they distort the whole perspective of his face. He won't say a word. He'll sit and listen. Sometimes he's listening to what you say, and when he does he has an uncanny ability to remember everything. Sometimes his mind is two or three thousand miles away and he isn't paying the slightest attention to what you're saying. It's disconcerting because you never know."

"He doesn't contribute to the conversation?"

"He sits and looks."

"Are he and his wife happy?"

"I suppose so. She dominates him but he doesn't realize it. She has the money. She likes to be the wife of an archaeologist. They travel around in various places where they can poke through ruins."

"She likes that?"

"Oh, she goes and pokes and learns a line of patter so she can get the reputation of being very highbrow with people who know nothing about the subject. But she always manages to spend plenty of time in Paris, London, Rome, Cairo, Rio, and places like that. While Jarrett is out exploring she'll go some place where she can wait while he's 'establishing headquarters.'

"There, now you know the whole setup, Mr. Mason."

Mason studied her. "If it should transpire that the bank should recover a judgment against your father and be able to show that this oil property is held in trust for the bank, it wouldn't affect Jarrett because he's married money. It wouldn't affect you because you have money. But it would seriously affect Hattie?"

"Well, I suppose so, if you want to put it *that* way, but there's also the family good name. Phoebe can support an archaeologist and loves doing it, but being married to the son of a bank thief is something else. I also have my own reputation to consider."

"And Hattie?"

"It would, of course, mean a great deal to Hattie."

"And Edison?" Mason asked.

"How do you mean?"

"Edison certainly has human intelligence. He must have realized that some day your father is going to die and that Hattie will inherit a very sizable amount of property."

"He isn't that kind."

"I'm not trying to say that he's marrying her because of that, but he must have realized that."

"Oh, I suppose he does."

"And that might make quite a difference to him."

She slowed the car, turned to regard the lawyer. "You *do* have the damnedest way of expressing things," she said.

"I take it," Mason said, abruptly changing the subject, "your brother Jarrett doesn't know anything about this?"

"He does now. I talked with Jarrett last night on the long-distance telephone."

"And told him about this?"

"Yes."

"Why the urgency?"

"Because," she said, "if I'm going to put up money to safeguard the estate, I expect the estate to pay me back. I wanted to be sure that anything I did had the approval of *all* the family."

"He gave his approval?"

"In a limited way," she said, and laughed bitterly.

"What's the limitation?"

"Oh, I guess I'm supposed to be selfish or something. Anyway, he told me to talk it over with Hattie, and that anything Hattie agreed to would be all right with him, but that before any money was actually paid over he wanted to know how much it was and how much of a contribution I was going to expect from him."

"And you told him?"

"Of course," she said caustically. "What he was angling for was for me to tell him to forget it, that I'd advance whatever was required and the estate could reimburse me after Dad died.

"But he was so damned obvious about it that I got mad and told him that I'd expect him to put up a third of whatever we had to pay."

"What did he say to that?"

"He didn't *say* much. That's not his way, but you could almost hear him thinking. Of course, he'd have to go to Phoebe to get the money and in order to do that he'd have to tell her what it was for.

"In a way I can see the thing from his angle. I'm supposed to be the selfish one in the family, but he's just as bad as I am. *He* didn't do anything to help care for the family. He married money and went off photographing ruins and digging into musty old graves.

"If he'd been decent about it, I might have put up the money; as it is he can dig up his own share. I hope he has imagination enough to lie to Phoebe, but I just don't give a damn."

"Well," Mason said, "that seems to give me a pretty fair picture."

She whipped the car savagely around a corner to the right, drove three swift blocks, then braked the car to a stop in front of a somewhat old-fashioned, two and a half story, rambling structure.

"This is it?" Mason asked.

"This is it."

"You've lived here some time?"

"I was born here," she said. "Now the thing is a white elephant, but we love it. Hattie has charge of it. She keeps it running somehow. Now let me tell you something else, Mr. Perry Mason. If you're going to sit there and look at me in that tone of voice, you and I aren't going to get along worth a damn.

"I don't take kindly to having people adopt a holier-than-thou attitude and intimating that I should have stayed home and sacrificed myself for the family, when I have a pair of gams that men notice and get excited over."

"They *do* get excited?" Mason asked.

She flashed him a defiant glance from her green eyes, then stretching her legs out in front of her, put her ankles together, whipped her skirt up as far as the tops of her stockings. "What do you think?" she asked, then added abruptly, "I'm afraid you're bringing out all the hell cat in me, Mr. Perry Mason. Come on, let's go in."

She opened the door and jumped to the sidewalk before Mason had the door on his side opened.

Together they walked up to the big front porch with wooden lattice work ornamenting the eaves in the architectural taste of a bygone generation.

Sylvia opened the front door, called out, "Yoo-hoo, company's coming. Everybody decent? Come on in, Mr. Mason."

She paused for a moment, holding the doorway open, said over her shoulder, half-apologetically, half-defiantly, "I'm sorry. I'm not usually an exhibitionist, and I'm not usually so nasty. Here's Hattie.

"Hattie, this is Mr. Perry Mason. My sister, Mr. Mason."

Hattie Bain seemed tired. There was a droop to her shoulders, a droop at the corners of her mouth, a worried look about the large, dark eyes set under a high forehead, surmounted by raven-black hair that was swept back in a style of plain severity.

She gave the lawyer her hand.

"I'm *so* glad you're working on this, Mr. Mason," she said. "We can't begin to tell you what a relief it is."

"How's Dad?" Sylvia asked.

"Not too good. He's badly upset. The medicine doesn't seem to be helping him much. Edison's here."

Mason saw Sylvia Atwood's face light up.

A slender, well-knit young man stepped out into the hallway.

"Hearing the sound of my name I thought I'd better flutter my wings," he said, smiling.

He came forward at once toward Mason, hand outstretched.

"This is Edison Doyle, Mr. Mason."

"Mr. Mason," Doyle said, shaking hands cordially, "it certainly is a pleasure to meet you. I've heard a lot about you and have followed many of your cases. I'm sorry that the thing which brings you here today is a potential misfortune for the family, but it's an unexpected honor."

"Glad to meet you," Mason said. "I understand you are an architect."

"Well, I have a license as an architect, and I have an office. I even have a *little* business."

Doyle's grin was good-natured and infectious.

Mason was conscious of the fact that both women were watching him. There was an indulgent something about Sylvia's mouth as though she might be saying to herself, "He really *is* a darling."

Hattie Bain's eyes left no misunderstanding as to her feelings in the matter, although back of the radiant devotion of her expression was something that could have been anxiety.

"Well, come on," Sylvia said to Mason. "Where's Dad, Hattie?"

"Up in his room."

"In bed?"

"No. He gets nervous when he's lying down. The doctor gave him medicine, but Dad's upset and can't seem to get himself under control. I'm terribly glad you could come, Mr. Mason. I think it will mean a lot."

Sylvia said, "Well, come on, let's put this show on the road."

She led the way through a living room, down a corridor.

"Dad had his study and bedroom upstairs," she said over her shoulder, "but after his heart got bad the doctor didn't want him to climb stairs, so we've put him back here on the ground floor."

She paused at a door and knocked.

"Come in," a man's voice called.

Sylvia opened the door, said, "Hello, Dad, how are you?"

She managed to put a note of breezy cordiality into her voice, a cheering confidence that brought an instant response from the white-haired man who was seated in a big reclining chair, propped up with pillows.

"Sylvia! I knew *you'd* be on the job."

"I've been on the job, Dad," she said. "I want you to meet Perry Mason, the famous lawyer."

"Excuse me if I don't get up," Bain said.

Mason strode across and shook hands. "Glad to know you, Mr. Bain."

Ned Bain's voice showed the fatigue brought on by excitement. "This is a real pleasure. I've heard so much about you. I never thought you'd be here. That's one thing about Sylvia, she gets the best—that's what I've always claimed, that it pays to get the best when you want either a doctor or a lawyer."

"Thank you," Mason said. "I'm not going to take up any of your time or bother you at all, Mr. Bain. We all feel that you should conserve your strength. I just wanted to tell you that I'm working on this situation and I think we're going to be able to clarify it."

"J.J.'s a crook," Bain said. "I used to like him a lot, but he fooled me."

"Don't worry about him. We'll take care of him."

Bain nodded. "I hope you do. I'm terribly worried about this thing. I want to leave my family well provided for. I know that I don't have too long. But I'd much rather they had self-respect than money. If we compromise with that crook it would look as though I'd been a party to that deal. The disgrace would remain long after I was gone. That's too great a price to pay for financial security, Mr. Mason."

Mason nodded.

"Where's Hattie?" Ned Bain asked Sylvia.

"She was right behind us."

Bain said, "I suppose Edison knows all about it?"

"Not through me," Sylvia said.

"Well, I suppose it can't be helped. After all, it is only fair, I suppose, to—"

Hattie Bain bustled into the room, said, "Your office is trying to get you on the telephone, Mr. Mason. They say it's terribly important."

"If you'll excuse me," Mason said, "I'll—"

"There's a phone right here," Bain said, indicating a little stand by the side of his chair. He pressed a button. A sliding shelf moved out, carrying a desk telephone. "This is an extension from the other room."

"Thanks. If it won't bother you I'll take it here," Mason said. "Apparently it's urgent."

He picked up the phone, glanced at Hattie Bain, and she said, "I'll go hang up the other phone, Mr. Mason. Sometimes you don't hear as well when both receivers are off."

Della Street's voice, sharp with excitement, came over the line, "Chief, Paul Drake's man telephoned. Can you find out what J.J. Fritch looks like? Give me a description quick? Paul Drake is waiting here."

Mason turned to Ned Bain. "I'm wondering," he said, "if you can give us a description of J.J. Fritch."

"Certainly," Bain said. "He's a slender man with high cheek-bones, a weather-beaten face, deep-set gray eyes, and has a characteristic stoop. He likes to wear broad-brimmed hats, Texas style. He's a little chap."

"How old?"

"Only around fifty-five, but he's stooped."

"What will he weigh?"

"Not over a hundred and thirty."

Mason relayed the description into the telephone, heard Della Street pass it on to Paul Drake.

"Hang on just a minute," Della Street said.

Mason stood holding the telephone.

Mason heard Paul Drake say, "Pass that on, if you will, Della," and then Drake's voice was on the line, "Hello, Perry."

"Hello, Paul."

"I guess we have the answer, Perry."

"What is it?"

"Your friend Brogan just left his apartment house. From your description, the man with him must be J.J. Fritch."

Mason said, "That means he must have gone to Brogan's apartment and—wait a minute, Paul. It probably means that Fritch *has an apartment in the same building, perhaps on the same floor, and—*"

"He does," Drake interrupted. "We've cheeked him. He's living in the apartment right across from Brogan."

"Right across the hall?" Mason asked.

"That's right. Right across the hall."

"Under what name?"

"Under the name of Frank Reedy."

"That means it's regular, orthodox blackmail," Mason said.

"That's all it ever was, just a regular shakedown racket. Brogan is putting up the front and pretending to be highly ethical. He's keeping Fritch in the background."

"Well," Mason said, "that's something. Have you got a tail on them?"

"That's right. I split it up. One of my operatives is trailing Fritch and the other one is following Brogan. Both had an idea as soon as the men walked out that we'd want to know something about the one who was with Brogan because of the Texas hat and the general setup. I had told them there was a Texas angle to the case and to report if anyone looking like a Texan around fifty-five or sixty came to visit Brogan."

"That's good work, Paul. If you need more men put them on the job. We want to find out what's going on."

"Okay, I'm keeping it covered."

"How did they seem, Paul? Could your men tell anything about the expressions?"

"They were both of them grinning, seemed to be enjoying some sort of a joke,"

"They probably are," Mason said. "Perhaps the joke will turn out to be on them."

Mason hung up the telephone, grinned reassuringly at Bain's anxious upturned face. "It's all right, Mr. Bain. It's coming along in good shape."

"Can you tell me why you wanted Fritch's description?"

"We've got him located."

A little twitch of excitement stirred Bain's form. "Where?" he said eagerly. "Where is the two-timing crook?"

"As a matter of fact," Mason said, "he has an apartment right across from the apartment of George Brogan. Fritch is registered under the name of Frank Reedy, and I don't think there's any question but what he has a lot of sound equipment in there so he can dub and duplicate sound recordings.

"What I think happened, Mr. Bain, is that Fritch engaged you in a long conversation dealing with cattle, talking about old times, and things of that sort."

Bain nodded. "I remember the occasion very clearly. We talked for about two hours," he said.

"And," Mason went on, "Fritch and Brogan fixed up a master recording from that conversation. They had that conversation transcribed so that they had everything before them in writing. Then they picked out certain of your answers that they wanted to use. Then Fritch went to a sound studio and asked questions that would fit in with his purpose and to which your answers would seem to be responsive. They had a tape recording of those questions, then with the aid of a crooked sound technician, they started splicing tape, leaving a good part of the conversation just the way it was, but interpolating a question asked by Fritch, tying it in with your answer to some perfectly innocuous question Fritch had asked at the time of the conversation. But, of course, Fritch's original question was cut out of the spool and the sinister question by him was inserted.

"After they'd fixed up this purely synthetic interview, they went ahead and dubbed it on to a tape. Naturally that tape showed no splices and apparently was a genuine recording."

Bain sighed. "I'm not supposed to get angry," he said. "If I do, it may kill me. I can pop out just like that, Mr. Mason."

Bain snapped bony fingers.

"I know," Mason said. "You must take it easy."

"The trouble is it isn't going to do any good for me to take it easy. Now what are they going to do with that recording?"

Mason said, "Frankly I don't think they'll do anything except try to blackmail you. If they *can't* do that they *might* try to make a deal with the bank.

"That's where Brogan enters into the picture. He can go to the bank as a private detective who has been digging around trying to unearth information that would be of value to the bank. He'll suggest to them that if they want to retain him at a fancy price he'll try and get evidence that will enable them to bring a suit against you."

"Of course," Bain said, "you understand, Mr. Mason, that I simply can't afford to have that happen, no matter what the price may be."

"Why not?" Mason asked. "It might be a good plan to air the whole thing in court."

Bain shook his head. "Just filing that suit," he said, "would completely ruin me. It would be picked up by the papers and reported all over the country. Everyone would feel that I had been Fritch's partner in that bank robbery. I simply can't afford to have anything like that happen. That would blacken the name of my family even more than paying those blackmailers something to get rid of them."

"But," Mason said, "you wouldn't ever get rid of them. You can see what's happened. They've got that master recording. They can keep making dubs from it. Brogan assured us that there was only one tape and that was the one we were listening to, but I've now definitely established that the one I was listening to was a copy."

Sylvia said, "Quit worrying about it, Dad. Leave these crooks to Mr. Mason. He'll find a way to fix them. Now you just leave things to him."

"That's what I'm going to do," Bain said. "However, I'd sure like to hear that recording and see if it's my voice."

"It's your voice, Dad," Sylvia Atwood said.

"I think it is," Mason told him. "But I don't think you need to be at all concerned about that. I feel certain we are going to spike their guns. They've secured your voice and then faked questions. I can tell you one thing, Mr. Bain. There isn't anything on that recording that is, in my opinion, at all incriminating. All of the incriminating statements are contained in the questions by J.J. Fritch. Your answers simply are to the effect that you're agreeing with him. I meet Brogan at his apartment at nine tomorrow to hear it again."

Bain's eyelids fluttered. He nodded, then his head drooped forward, his eyes remained closed. His breathing was slow and regular.

Hattie Bain, who had returned to the room, placed her finger to her lips in a gesture for silence.

Slowly they tiptoed out of the room and closed the door behind them, leaving Ned Bain sleeping in the chair, propped up by pillows.

"The doctor gave him some heart medicine," Hattie said. "Something that's supposed to make it easier on his heart. It relaxes the capillaries. He also gave him some sort of a sedative to keep him quiet because he said Dad was terribly nervous, and the nervousness was having just as bad an effect as an overdose of excitement.

"The trouble was Dad was so worked up he simply couldn't get to sleep. Talking with you has done a lot for him, Mr. Mason. I could see him quieting right while he was talking with you. Couldn't you, Sylvia?"

"Yes, indeed," she said.

"Well," Mason said, "I'll be getting on back to my office. Do you want to join me at nine o'clock tomorrow morning, Mrs. Atwood?"

"Yes, indeed. That's pretty early, however. Suppose I meet you—well, now wait a minute. It's going to be rather difficult for me to drive all the way uptown and then back to Brogan's apartment. Suppose I come directly to Mr. Brogan's apartment? How will that be?"

"That's fine," Mason said. "I'll meet you there."

"At nine o'clock tomorrow morning," she said. "I'll drive you back, Mr. Mason."

"Hey," Edison Doyle said, "you don't need to do that, Sylvia. I'm headed back uptown anyway and I'd certainly like to drive Mr. Mason up to his office. I'd deem it a pleasure."

Sylvia hesitated. "Well, perhaps I *should* stay here with Dad and see what I can do if he wakes up. You won't mind, Mr. Mason?"

"Certainly not," Mason said. "I hope we've been able to reassure your father."

"Oh, I'm satisfied you have," Hattie interposed. "Dad was, of course, terribly worried. There's something there in the background that we don't know, something that he knows about J.J., something that causes him to fear J.J. I think Fritch must be a very desperate man and Dad must know it."

"Can you imagine him doing anything so utterly reprehensible as ringing up Mr. Bain?" Doyle asked.

Mason said, "That shows that his back is against the wall."

"I'm afraid I don't understand," Hattie said, genuinely perplexed.

"Don't you see," Sylvia explained, "as soon as Mr. Mason entered the picture they felt certain they were going to be defeated, so then J.J. telephoned Dad, trying to frighten him, not caring a thing about the consequences."

"He should be given a damn good thrashing," Edison Doyle said. "I understand you've proven now that he and this private detective are in cahoots."

"They must be," Mason said. "Fritch has an apartment directly across the hall from Brogan. He's going under the name of Frank Reedy. I imagine they're getting hot under the collar."

"Just what can be done?"

"If we can get the evidence," Mason said, "the evidence that I hope I'm going to get, we can have them arrested for conspiracy."

"Dad wouldn't want that," Hattie said quickly. "He wouldn't want any publicity at all."

"Well, come on," Doyle said. "I'll get you back to your office, Mr. Mason. My chariot's outside. It's not the latest or the best, but it gets you there."

Mason said good-bye to the others, followed Doyle out and jumped in the five-year-old car as Doyle held the door open for him.

Doyle, getting around behind the wheel, said, "There's one thing I don't understand about the legal aspect of this case, Mr. Mason."

"What's that?" the lawyer asked, as the car eased away from the curb.

"Just how are they going to identify that tape recording?"

"It has to be done by the testimony of J.J. Fritch," Mason said. "In other words, Fritch would get on the stand and swear that he had this conversation and that for his own protection he had made a tape recording."

"And Fritch is a crook?"

"Undoubtedly."

"And a blackmailer?"

"Undoubtedly."

"And if anything happened that Fritch had to skip out and wasn't there to identify that conversation it couldn't be used?"

"That's right," Mason said. "The tape recording would have to be identified. Fritch would have to testify that it was a recording of a genuine conversation that he'd had with Ned Bain."

"And on cross-examination Fritch would have to admit that he'd robbed the bank?"

"As I understand the facts, that's right."

"It would seem to me you could rip him wide open on cross-examination."

"I can," Mason said, "but the point is that the filing of the case would result in a lot of unfavorable publicity. I think that's what's worrying Mr. Bain."

"That's so," Doyle admitted. "I don't suppose Bain is worrying so much for himself. He's thinking about the daughters—a couple of fine girls—and to have that thing hanging over their heads—No, we just can't let that happen, Mr. Mason, no matter what we have to do."

Mason nodded.

"A couple of fine girls like that!" Doyle repeated. "Gosh, you don't find them any better anywhere in the world.

"There's Hattie, she's the most loyal, considerate, self-effacing girl you can imagine. And—well, no one needs a press agent for Sylvia Atwood."

Mason smiled and nodded.

"She's a real beauty," Doyle said, "and full of fun and—there's something so alive, so vital about her. You feel like a new man when you're around her.

"I don't mind telling you, Mr. Mason, that I've probably taken life a little too seriously. I've had my nose stuck too close to the drafting board. That's probably a good way to lay the foundation for architectural skill, but it's a darned poor way to start life."

"I think you'll find it'll pay dividends," Mason said.

"Oh, I suppose so, but when you see what happens to people who take life too seriously, and contrast them with a girl like Sylvia—I don't know, Mr. Mason, I think life, like money, was meant to be spent. You can't hoard money and ever get any good out of it. And life was meant to be lived. Somehow—it's hard to express, but I don't think there's anything more perishable than the seconds that are ticked off by the second hand on a watch. You can't save them. You have to spend them. You have to live them."

"It's not quite as simple as that," Mason said. "A person has to prepare himself. You have to lay a foundation for life. The time you spend in study is an investment, as good as money in a bank."

"Yes, I suppose so," Doyle observed, and lapsed into silence.

After a moment Mason said, "I suppose the girls confided in you as soon as this came up?"

"Hattie did," Doyle said. "She's terribly conscientious. She—well, if there was anything that was going to affect the family, any old scandal or anything, she wanted me to know it before—well, before I committed myself."

He laughed nervously.

"I wasn't trying to pry into your private affairs," Mason said.

"No, no, not at all. I'm glad to have an opportunity to explain matters. I'd do anything for those two girls, Mr. Mason, anything."

"For the *two* girls," Mason said.

There was a moment's silence, then Doyle nodded. "That's right, Mr. Mason."

After that he was silent until he had deposited the lawyer in front of his office building and squeezed the attorney's hand in a parting gesture of cordiality.

"It was wonderful meeting you, Mr. Mason, simply wonderful. It's an experience I won't ever forget. Having you in our corner gives one a feeling of complete invincibility."

Mason laughed. "Don't overestimate me," he said. "I think we're making progress, but that's the most I can say at the moment."

CHAPTER 6

It was almost eight-fifty the next morning when Mason parked his car in front of the apartment house. Della Street opened the door on her side, jumped to the sidewalk.

"You want me to go up with you?" she asked, as Mason walked around the car to join her.

Mason nodded.

"And just what am I supposed to do?"

"Keep your eyes and ears open," Mason said.

"How are you going to explain to Mr. Brogan the fact that I'm with you?"

Mason said, "We don't have to explain anything to Brogan. From now on he's going to be on the defensive."

"I take it I'm to be a witness?"

"That's right."

"But you have Sylvia Atwood."

"That's right. I want a witness I can depend on."

"You don't think you can depend on her?"

"I don't know," Mason said. "Come on, let's go up. I see that Sylvia is already here. That's her car parked up ahead."

Della looked at her wrist watch. "She's early."

"Not too early. It'll take us two or three minutes to get up in the elevator. Come on, let's go."

They entered the apartment house, took the elevator, walked down the corridor. Della Street, who was a step in advance, said, "There's a note here, Chief. It's addressed to you."

Mason looked over her shoulder.

An envelope had been fastened to the door with a thumbtack. The envelope was addressed simply in red crayon, "Mr. Perry Mason."

Della glanced back over her shoulder and the lawyer nodded.

She pulled out the thumbtack, opened the unsealed envelope, pulled out the note. She held it so they could both read it.

It was scrawled in pencil.

Mr. Mason:

Occasionally I indulge in a poker game with some of the boys. It happens tonight is the night. We're starting early, about ten o'clock I understand, and I'm hoping to be finished in ample time to keep our appointment. If, however, I should be a few minutes late please go on in and make yourself at home. I'm leaving the apartment unlocked so you can go on in and wait. I promise you that if I'm not there promptly at nine I won't be over ten minutes late.

George Brogan

Mason regarded the note thoughtfully, then he carefully folded it, put it back in the envelope, used his cigarette lighter to look for the exact hole which had been made by the thumbtack.

"You're suspicious?" Della Street asked.

"It's a trap," Mason said. "I want to get this back in the original hole made by the thumbtack so no one can prove we've read it. We—oh-oh."

"What is it?" Della Street asked.

"Two holes here," Mason said. "Someone else has taken it off, read it and put it back, but didn't realize the necessity for putting it back in the original hole."

"So what do we do?"

"Well," Mason said, "we don't make a third hole, that's certain. We put it back but—I guess Brogan was smart enough to know I might do just that, so he made two thumbtack holes so I couldn't say I hadn't read it. And since he's gone to that trouble and I'm trapped, I may as well put the note in my pocket."

Mason viciously jabbed the thumbtack into the panel of the door, put the envelope and note in his pocket.

"And we go in?" Della Street asked.

Mason shook his head.

"Why not?"

"I tell you it's a trap. He wants us to go in and search the apartment. He's too damned anxious."

"Why?"

"Nothing for our good," Mason said. "Whatever reason will be for his good."

"Such as what? What could he possibly gain by—?"

Mason said, "Suppose we go in the apartment and find someone has smashed open the safe?"

"So we wait right here?"

"I don't know," Mason said. "Having left the apartment unlocked, he can always claim we went in and—we'll be waiting right here when he comes, and we'll tell him just what we think of his traps and—wait a minute, Sylvia's up here somewhere. She—"

He broke off as a jarring thud from the interior of the apartment shook the floor under them.

"What was that?" Della Street asked, startled.

"I don't know," Mason said. "It sounded as if someone had been—"

He broke off as a woman's terrified scream came from the interior of the apartment.

Della Street instinctively raised a gloved hand to the doorknob, started to turn it.

Mason slapped her hand away.

"Chief, someone's in trouble in there. Someone's screaming."

Mason nodded.

"But, Chief, we can't leave that person in danger. That was a scream of terror. That—"

The door was abruptly jerked open from the inside. A woman's hurrying figure started to dash out into the corridor, then straightened in a rigidity of dismay as she saw Mason and Della Street standing on the threshold.

"Well, Mrs. Atwood," Mason said calmly, "you seem to have gone exploring."

"Oh, it's you!" she exclaimed. "Thank heavens. Oh, quick. Good Lord—"

"What is it?" Mason asked.

"J.J. Fritch. He's been killed."

"How do you know?"

"His body was in the liquor closet. It toppled out on its face."

Mason jerked a handkerchief from his pocket, held it over the palm of his hand, grabbed the knob of the door, pulled the door shut. He said to Sylvia Atwood, "You're wearing gloves. Did you have them off when you were in there?"

She shook her head. Her face had gone white under the make-up, causing the rouge to flare into bizarre prominence even there in the dim light of the hall. "I had my gloves on all the time."

"It was Fritch?" Mason asked.

She nodded.

"You're sure he was dead?"

"Good heavens, yes. He toppled forward—"

"How's he dressed?"

"He isn't dressed."

"Naked?"

"He has on underwear. A sleeveless undershirt and shorts."

"No socks?"

She shook her head.

"No shoes?"

Again she shook her head.

Della Street looked at Mason anxiously. "Shouldn't we—?"

Mason shook his head. "This is a trap. We've walked into it. Let's try to get out of it."

Still with the handkerchief over his palm, he gently tried the door of the apartment directly behind them and across the hall from the door of Brogan's apartment.

The knob turned smoothly. The apartment door opened.

Mason turned back to the two young women.

"Listen," he said, "I want you to get this and get it straight. Brogan will show up any minute now. He'll be all flustered and in a hurry, claiming that he was detained in a poker game. I want you to tell him that I am downstairs parking the car. His natural inference will be that we all three came together, that I stopped in front of the apartment house to let you two girls out, that I then cruised around to find a parking place for the car, that I'll be up immediately."

"Won't he question us on details?" Della Street asked.

"I'll show up before he gets a chance to question you," Mason said, "provided you do *just* as I say."

"Della, here's the note that was on the door. Be holding that in your hand. Have the paper open as though you had just read it. That will give you an excuse to know that the door is open and unlocked."

She nodded.

"As soon as you have told him that I'm parking the car," Mason said, "turn the knob and walk in just casually and naturally, saying you were about to do so anyway because you'd read the note addressed to me, that I'll be right up."

Della Street nodded.

"Now then," Mason said to Sylvia Atwood, "while that is taking place you'll have an opportunity to step into the background. Don't turn so that you face this apartment, but put your hand behind your back, grope until you find the bell on this apartment. Ring it twice. Two short, quick rings. Then follow Della and George Brogan into the apartment. Manipulate it so you'll be the last one in—"

"Won't Brogan stand to one side for us two to enter first and—"

"See that he doesn't. Brogan is a crook and a blackmailer. He never was a gentleman. He isn't too concerned with the niceties of etiquette."

"And what will you do?"

Mason said, "There's one chance in a hundred I may have that master spool of tape before Brogan turns up. I'll hear your signal. I'll give you just about three seconds to get through the door, after I hear the two rings, then I'll slip out into the corridor, close this door behind me and ring Brogan's bell, or I *may* be able to get here just as you're closing the door and come on in. In that way Brogan can't prove where I've been. Perhaps he'll think I really was parking the car. Now, have you folks got that straight?"

"I have," Della Street said.

Sylvia Atwood said, "I don't understand just how—"

"You don't have to," Della said briskly. "I'll tell you what to do. Do exactly what Mr. Mason says. Go ahead, Chief."

Mason slipped open the door of Fritch's apartment, which had been rented under the name of Frank Reedy, and closed the door behind him.

The drapes were drawn across the windows. The lights were on. In a corner of the room a television set was flickering a commercial.

Mason slipped through the living room, entered a bedroom.

Here again drapes were drawn across the windows. The bed was freshly made and apparently had not been slept in. A dressing gown was thrown across a chair by the bedside. There were also bedroom slippers neatly arranged under the chair.

Mason looked in the bathroom. It was entirely in order, but here again an electric light was on and a shade was pulled.

Mason retraced his steps, pushed open a door into the kitchenette.

Immediately he sensed a peculiar situation. Every shelf was loaded to the brim with canned goods. Mason opened the icebox. It was filled with food. At one end of the kitchen a deep-freeze unit had been installed, a huge affair some seven feet in length.

Mason opened the lid and whistled in surprise. It was jammed to the brim with frozen foods, meat wrapped in packages and labeled, ice cream, frozen strawberries, frozen cherries, package after package of frozen vegetables, packages of biscuit dough which needed only to be put in the oven and baked, pound after pound of butter, several pies and cakes.

Mason lowered the lid, snapped the latch into place.

Apparently J.J. Fritch had been prepared for a siege. He had been in a position to close the door of his apartment and completely retire from the world. There would have been no necessity for him to go out. He could have remained in hiding for weeks or months as the occasion might require.

Mason left the kitchen, returned to the living room, opened the door of a huge closet.

It was well filled with clothing, shoes and sound recording equipment.

Mason tried the closets in the bedroom, being careful whenever he touched anything to have a handkerchief over his hand.

The bedroom closet held a conventional array of men's clothing.

Mason was just about to try a dresser drawer when the bell of the apartment gave two quick, sharp rings.

Mason dashed to the door leading to the hallway, stood there and listened.

He heard feminine voices, heard the booming of a masculine voice. He waited about three seconds, then eased the door open.

The door of the apartment across the way was just closing. Sylvia Atwood was standing in the doorway, gently pushing it shut.

Mason jumped into the corridor, pulled the door of Fritch's apartment shut behind him, pushed on the door of the Brogan apartment, said to Sylvia Atwood, "Well, I guess I'm not late after all."

George Brogan grinned at Mason, walked on across to the windows, pulled back the drapes letting in morning sunlight.

Brogan was a disreputable-looking spectacle. His face had a shadow of dark stubble. The collar of his shirt was wilted down in front where his perspiring chin had been resting against the top of the collar. The skin of his face had that peculiar oily appearance which in some men is an indication of a sleepless night. His eyes were weary and a little bloodshot. There was an odor of alcohol on his breath.

"I'm sorry," he said. "Did you get my note, Mason?"

Mason looked blank.

Della Street said, "Here it is, Chief. It was on the door," and handed Mason the note.

Brogan looked inquiringly at Della Street.

"Miss Street, my confidential secretary," Mason said. "I brought her with me this morning. She came up ahead of me."

"Oh," Brogan said, and then, bowing, muttered the conventional formula of pleasure at making her acquaintance, but his eyes, anxious and furtive, rested apprehensively on Mason's face as Mason read the note.

Brogan waited until he was certain Mason had finished reading, then said, "I'm terribly sorry, Mason. I like to be right on the dot. When I make an appointment I like to keep it, but—well, as you can see, I didn't even stop to get a shave. I dashed up here, stopped long enough to just gulp down a cup of coffee and a couple of eggs. I was getting a terrific headache and wouldn't have been good for anything without some coffee. As it is, I'm only—" he looked at his watch—"five minutes late.

"You know how it is, Mason. I intended to get away from the game early, but I started losing pretty heavily and got mad and began plunging. Then I began to recuperate. Got my losses back and a little more to boot, and—well, when a man gets in that position he keeps thinking—well, just one hand more. And, of course, the others are sore that you're winning. They want an opportunity to get it back. They don't want to see you get up and take their money out of the game.

"So I kept postponing my departure for one hand at a time until finally I just had time enough to make a dash for it. I'm terribly sorry. Won't you folks sit down. I trust you young women will pardon my appearance.

"Now I know what you're thinking, Mason. I know you're thinking that the fault wasn't with that machine yesterday, but that something had gone wrong and the recording had been erased. I'm going to play that tape for you once more so you'll see that nothing has happened to it. First, if you'll pardon me. I'll put on some strong black coffee in the kitchen. I've been up all night and I—"

Brogan started for the kitchen.

Sylvia Atwood flashed Mason a warning glance.

Brogan stepped through the door, then suddenly stopped and stood rigid.

"What's the matter?" Mason asked after a moment.

Brogan slowly turned, closed the door behind him, came to stand directly in front of Mason. His eyes were cold, hard and accusing.

"What the hell's the idea, Mason?" he asked.

"What are you talking about?" Mason asked.

Brogan said, "I left that note on the door before I went out. The apartment was open all night. You came here early. You got that note. You—I think under the circumstances this is the thing to do."

Brogan walked over to the telephone, jerked up the receiver, dialed Operator and said, "Get me police headquarters quick. There's been a murder and I'm holding three people here. One of them is probably the murderer."

CHAPTER 7

Sergeant Holcomb of Homicide could, when he chose and without apparent effort, be exceedingly nasty, sarcastic and disagreeable.

This time he was in rare form.

"I tell you," Mason said angrily, "I can't wait around here all day. I've been here two hours now."

Sergeant Holcomb, who had commandeered the manager's apartment and was holding all witnesses incommunicado, had taken his time about sending for Perry Mason. Now his eyes glittered ominously.

"Don't pull that line with me," he said. "It's overworked. You've done it too much. You've discovered too many corpses."

"I didn't discover this corpse," Mason said.

"That's what you say."

"Does anyone say I did?"

"*I'm* asking the questions."

"Go on and ask them then."

"Did you know J.J. Fritch in his lifetime?"

"I never met the man that I know of."

"What do you know about the manner in which is body was discovered?"

"George Brogan started out for the kitchen to put on some coffee, stopped, turned around and called the police."

"What were you doing here?"

"I had an appointment with Brogan."

"About what?"

"A matter of business."

"Tell me about it."

Mason shook his head.

"Why not?"

"It's confidential."

"Nothing's confidential in a murder case."

"That's where you and I have a difference of opinion. We've had them before and I dare say we'll have them again."

"I understand you told Brogan you were deaf and had to wear a hearing aid."

"Wrong again."

"You were wearing a hearing aid."

"No. That's a pocket-size wire recorder. The microphone is held against my temple. If Brogan thought it was a hearing aid that was his mistake."

"Let's see it."

"There's nothing on it now. I hadn't switched it on today. I was waiting until my conversation with George Brogan—"

"Let's see it."

Mason took the device from his pocket, passed it over.

Sergeant Holcomb examined it for a few minutes, then opened his brief case and dropped it in. "You'll get this back after it's been examined. I'm not taking your word for anything."

"There's nothing on it today."

"What was on it yesterday?"

"That's my business, or rather my client's business."

"I can find out," Holcomb threatened.

"Then do so, by all means."

"Brogan tells me he left a note on the door for you."

Mason nodded.

"Your secretary, Della Street, had the note in her possession."

"What did *she* tell you?" Mason asked.

Holcomb merely grinned and said, "I'm asking *you* the questions now."

"Very well," Mason said, tightening his lips, his face granite hard. "Go ahead and ask them."

"And remember you're an attorney at law, an officer of the court," Holcomb went on. "Don't you think you can get smart and arbitrarily withhold information."

Mason said, "I am sworn by my oath of office to protect my clients. I am going to protect them to the best of my ability. Don't think you can use your authority to browbeat information out of me that I don't think it's proper to give."

"Did your client murder J.J. Fritch?" Holcomb asked sneeringly.

"How the hell do I know," Mason said.

"How's that?" Holcomb asked in surprise.

"I said I wouldn't know."

"Why?" Holcomb asked, his eyes narrowing. "What makes you suspicious?"

"I'm not suspicious."

"Well, your statement implies there's a possibility a client of yours murdered Fritch."

"Certainly there's a possibility."

"You don't know?"

"I don't know."

"Why?"

"For one thing I haven't been permitted to talk with my client. I haven't been permitted to talk with anyone."

"Do you think I'm dumb enough to leave all the witnesses together so they can fix up a story that will account for all of the facts and leave me holding the sack? I wasn't born yesterday."

"Do you think I'm dumb enough to give you information that may betray the interests of a client before I've talked with my client?" Mason retorted.

Holcomb's face darkened. "You'll either give me the information or you'll wish you had."

"Go ahead, ask your questions."

"What were you doing here?"

"I had an appointment."

"With whom?"

"George Brogan."

"When?"

"Nine o'clock."

"What time did you get here?"

"I didn't look at my watch."

"Brogan left a note on the door."

"So I understand."

"Your secretary says she read it."

"Thank you."

"For what?"

"For telling me what my secretary said."

"I'm not telling you all she said."

"Then I'll withdraw my thanks."

"This isn't going to get you anywhere."

"It isn't going to get *you* anywhere."

"When did you first know Fritch had been murdered?"

"I still don't know he's been murdered."

"I told you so."

"I heard you."

"You mean you're not going to take my word?"

"I didn't say that."

"You intimated it."

Mason shrugged his shoulders and lit a cigarette.

"When did you last see J.J. Fritch alive?"

"I haven't seen him alive."

"When did you first see his body?"

"I haven't seen his body."

"What are your relations with Mrs. Sylvia Atwood?"

"She's my client."

"When did she get here?"

"I don't know."

"By here I mean to Brogan's apartment."

"I don't know."

"When did she tell you she got here?"

"I haven't had an opportunity to question her."

"That isn't what I asked you."

"That's what I told you."

"When did she tell you she got to the Brogan apartment?"

"I haven't had an opportunity to question her."

"I'm asking you for a certain specific piece of information."

"I'm giving you a certain specific piece of information."

"When did your secretary get here?"

"I haven't had an opportunity to talk with her."

"She came with you, didn't she?"

"I haven't had an opportunity to question her."

"She isn't your client, she's your secretary."

"How do I know she isn't my client? How do I know what you're going to do? You're crazy enough to charge her with first-degree murder."

"By God, Mason," Holcomb said, jumping to his feet, "I've got nerve enough to charge *you* with first-degree murder, and don't think I haven't."

"That's a threat?"

"You're damn right," Holcomb shouted, "that's a threat. I'll do it."

"Very well," Mason said, "in view of the statement you have just made I refuse to make any more statements until I have an opportunity to consult with counsel."

"With counsel?" Holcomb yelled. "You're a lawyer, and a damn good one, even if I hate to admit it."

"A lawyer," Mason said, "should never be his own client. If I'm going to be charged with murder I must have the advice of counsel."

"Well, how do I know whether you're going to be charged with murder or not?"

"You said you were going to."

"I said I could."

"You said you would."

"Well, I will if I think the facts warrant it."

"Do the facts warrant it?"

"Hell, I don't know."

"Then," Mason said, "I don't know whether I care to make any statement. I've told you that I had an appointment with Brogan for nine o'clock, that I came here to keep that appointment. I might have been a few minutes early. I might have been a few minutes late. I just don't recall looking at my watch. I don't even know if my watch is right. I understand Brogan left a note on the door telling me to go on in and sit down. I was delayed in getting to the apartment. As I entered the apartment I saw that my secretary, Della Street, had gone on in, that Brogan was following her, and that Sylvia Atwood was following Brogan. I was there in time to bring up the rear of the procession and close the door of the apartment behind us.

"Almost immediately Brogan explained that he had been engaged in an all-night poker game and had only stopped to grab a cup of coffee and a couple of eggs, that he felt pretty rocky, that he was sorry to be a few minutes late. I didn't look at my watch to check his statement, but I assumed from what he said that it was then a few minutes after nine o'clock."

"Then you yourself were late getting there," Holcomb charged.

Mason said nothing.

"Did you go directly up to Brogan's apartment when you left your car?"

"When I left my car?"

"Yes."

"Yes."

Holcomb frowned. "There's something funny about this, something that doesn't dovetail."

Mason shrugged his shoulders.

"You went directly to the Brogan apartment?"

"To the outer door, yes. Where did you expect me to go?"

Holcomb said, "You had to find a parking place for your car. The women went up first."

Mason yawned.

"Didn't they?" Holcomb asked.

Mason smiled. "I've made my statement, Sergeant Holcomb. In view of the fact that you have announced that you intend to file a first-degree murder charge against me I do not intend to make any further statement except in the presence of an attorney. I think my statement covers the ground sufficiently so that no important item of information that would assist in any way in carrying out your investigations has been withheld from you. I do not propose to tell you anything that might be considered the betrayal of a professional confidence."

"You can't tell us the nature of your business with Brogan?"

"I won't tell you."

"You can't tell us whether Mrs. Atwood was your client?"

"I can."

"Was she?"

"Yes."

"What were you doing for her?"

"Attending to a business matter."

"What sort of a business matter?"

Mason shrugged his shoulders.

"Brogan tells us it had to do with a tape recording."

"Does he indeed?"

"He says he looked for that tape recording and can't find it. He thinks you must have taken it."

"Indeed."

"Did you take a tape recording out of Brogan's apartment?"

"No."

"Did you know J.J. Fritch had the apartment across the hall under the name of Frank Reedy?"

"You mean he had the apartment directly across from George Brogan?" Mason asked, surprise in his voice.

"Yes."

Mason raised his eyebrows and whistled.

"Evidently you didn't know it then."

Mason said nothing.

"Well," Holcomb said, "go on and talk."

"I've talked."

"You haven't answered my questions."

"I don't intend to answer all of your questions. I have to draw the line."

"Well, tell me where you draw it," Holcomb said. "Let's get it straight for the record."

Mason said, "I draw a very sharp line of demarcation, Sergeant Holcomb. Your questions resolve themselves into two main categories."

"All right," Holcomb said, "what are they?"

"The questions that I choose to answer and the questions that I choose not to answer. The one classification I am quite willing to answer, the other I am not."

Holcomb's face reddened. "That's a hell of an attitude for an attorney at law to take."

"Isn't it?" Mason said, smiling. "What attitude would you suggest, Sergeant?"

"I'd suggest that you answer questions or you may find yourself in a hell of a predicament."

"You've already outlined that to me. You have even gone so far as to specify the predicament," Mason said, "that is, that I will be charged with first-degree murder. Now then, Sergeant, I feel that I have granted you every consideration and every courtesy. I have been kept waiting here while other witnesses have been interrogated. I think your ruling that no one could leave the apartment house is completely, utterly asinine. I am an attorney at law. I have an office here in the city. I can be found there whenever you want me. Now I'm going to get up and walk right out of here."

"That's what you think."

"I repeat," Mason said, "I am going to get up and walk right out of here unless I am forcibly restrained. If I am forcibly restrained it will only be because I am under arrest. If I am under arrest I want a charge to be preferred and then I want an opportunity to secure bail."

"You don't get bail for first-degree murder."

"That's fine. Then accuse me of first-degree murder."

"I'm not ready to."

"In that case," Mason said, "I'm walking right out of here, Sergeant. When you get ready to charge me, you know where to find me."

Mason got up and started for the door.

"Sit down," Holcomb shouted. "I'm not done with you."

"I'm done with you," Mason said and opened the door of the apartment.

"Hold him," Holcomb shouted.

A uniformed officer grabbed Mason by the arms.

"Bring him back," Holcomb said.

Mason said, "If you want to charge me with first-degree murder, Sergeant Holcomb, I'm here ready to be charged. If you want to put me under arrest, take me to headquarters. If you forcibly restrain me without putting me under arrest, or if you arrest me without charging me with crime, I'm going to sue you for false arrest and for assault. Now make up your mind which you want."

The officer dropped his hands to his sides, looked perplexedly at Sergeant Holcomb.

"Hold him," Holcomb said. "He can't pull that stuff."

"Are you charging me with anything?" Mason asked.

"I'll tell you one thing," Holcomb blazed. "Your story doesn't check with the other stories I've heard. *I* think you were in Brogan's apartment and then backed out again."

"I've told you repeatedly," Mason said, "that I had just entered Brogan's apartment on the heels of Brogan and the two young women."

"For the *first* time?"

"For the first time today. I was here yesterday."

"I think you're lying."

"Go to hell," Mason said and started for the door. "You'll either charge me or let me go. I won't tell you another thing."

The officer took a step after him.

Sergeant Holcomb abruptly changed his mind. He said wearily, "Oh, let him go," and sank back into his chair.

CHAPTER 8

Paul Drake slid into his favorite position in the big overstuffed leather chair in Mason's office. His body was cross-ways in the chair, the knees were draped over one rounded arm, the other was supporting the small of his back.

The detective raised his long arms, clasped his fingers back of his head, crossed his ankles.

"Go ahead," Mason said. "Give us the low-down, Paul."

"J.J. Fritch was killed by repeated stabs with an ice pick," Drake said. "There was very little external bleeding. Quite an intensive internal hemorrhage because two of the stabs penetrated the heart."

"How many wounds in all?"

"Eight."

"Someone wanted to make a good job of it."

"Apparently. Of course, with a small weapon like an ice pick—"

"Did they recover the ice pick?"

"Not yet."

"Was there an old-fashioned icebox in Brogan's apartment?"

"No, there wasn't. Brogan used an electric icebox and had ice cubes for his drinks. So did Fritch. Police aren't absolutely certain the weapon was an ice pick, but they think it was."

Mason's eyes narrowed.

"I'll tell you something else that hasn't occurred to the police—as yet," Drake went on.

"What?"

"The Bain household has an electric icebox, but it also has an old-fashioned ice chest on the back porch. Ned Bain sometimes has to have ice packs. They use about fifty pounds a day."

"Holcomb hasn't been out to the Bains' yet?"

"No."

"Della's out there now," Mason said.

"Perhaps she'd better look for the ice pick," Paul said.

Mason was silent for a few minutes.

"When was the murder committed, Paul?"

"Apparently between midnight and three o'clock in the morning, some time in there. The autopsy surgeon says he's positive it wasn't before midnight and he's positive it wasn't after three in the morning. That's the best he can do."

Mason's eyes narrowed thoughtfully.

"Where were you last night between midnight and three o'clock this morning, Perry?"

"In bed."

"That's what comes of being a bachelor. You should get married. As it is, you haven't any alibi. You only have your unsupported word."

Mason said, "The apartment house has a man on duty at the desk twenty-four hours a day."

"Would he have seen you if you went out?"

"I assume so."

"And when you came back?"

Mason nodded.

"He's probably being interrogated."

"You mean they're serious in thinking that *I* killed the man?" Mason asked incredulously.

"Well," Drake said, "here's the dope. Brogan has a perfect alibi."

"How perfect? It's going to have to be completely ironclad before I'll believe it. The whole thing looks too much like a setup to suit me. That poker game was *too* opportune. I think Brogan killed him."

Drake shook his head. "I tell you he has an alibi. He started playing poker at ten o'clock at night. He didn't leave until five o'clock in the morning. He had been losing heavily. At five o'clock he had to go out and raise some money. He was gone about half or three-quarters of an hour, came back, got in the game, and about eight o'clock kept trying to make a breakaway, claiming that he had an appointment on a very important business matter at nine o'clock, that he had to get shaved and had to change his shirt.

"When did he leave?"

"No one knows exactly, but it was somewhere around eight-thirty. He went and had breakfast and got up to the apartment just as Della Street and Sylvia Atwood were standing there. What did Della tell them, Perry?"

"Nothing," Mason said. "She adopted the position that she was my secretary, that under the law any information she might have affecting the rights of a client was confidential, that because she didn't know all of the details of the business I was transacting there, she might inadvertently disclose something that would be inimical to the best interests of the client I was representing, and which would in the nature of things be confidential. Therefore, she refused to make *any* statements whatever."

"Good girl," Drake said. "I understand Holcomb really gave her a going-over."

"Apparently he did. He tried everything under the sun. Della simply sat and smiled at him and told him that if she could first talk with me she'd be very glad to then disclose any information she had which was not confidential, but until she could talk with me she didn't know what information was confidential, and therefore she would tell him nothing except that she got up in the morning, dressed and waited for me to pick her up, that I picked her up at the appointed time. She won't even tell them what time that was."

Drake nodded. "What about Sylvia Atwood?"

"Sylvia Atwood," Mason said, "was the first one questioned. She told her story and Holcomb let her go. I got her on the phone and told her I wanted to see her, but she hasn't come in as yet."

"Did you interview her over the telephone?"

"Only generally. Della's checking exactly what was said."

"I assume you asked Sylvia what she told Holcomb?"

Mason nodded.

"What did she tell you?"

Mason said, "She gave me the story she'd given Brogan, that she came up to the apartment, that she found Della Street at the door reading a note, that the note said Brogan might be detained, that the door was open and we were to go in. Della Street didn't want to go in but Sylvia Atwood said, 'Why not.'"

"You weren't there at the time?"

"She said that I was parking the car," Mason went on, "and was coming up later. Brogan arrived while she and Della were talking things over, and that I was following right on Brogan's heels. She didn't notice the time in particular."

Drake said, "The officers found someone who has an apartment on the same floor that swears a woman screamed in one of the apartments a little before nine o'clock. The witness thinks the scream came from the Brogan apartment. The tenants in the apartment below heard a heavy thud in Brogan's apartment and the sound of a woman screaming. That was shortly *before* nine o'clock. They fix the time because they were waiting for a nine o'clock radio program.

"A witness in a ground floor apartment saw Mrs. Atwood trying to park her car and having the devil of a time getting it backed into a small parking space between two cars. Then the owner of the car that was parked behind the place she was trying to get in came out, saw her predicament, spoke to her, telling her he was pulling out.

"He pulled out and Mrs. Atwood backed in. The witness says the time was eight-thirty."

"Eight-thirty!" Mason exclaimed.

"That's right, eight-thirty."

"What about the man who drove out and gave her a chance to park?"

"He thinks it was about eight-forty. He drove uptown and reached his office at five of nine. It's a good fifteen minute drive at that hour."

Mason thought that over.

"Now then," Drake went on, "it looks as though your friend Brogan really came clean with the police."

"What do you mean?"

"He told them the exact nature of your business with him."

"The hell he did," Mason said.

"That's right. They asked him and he had no alternative but to tell them. At least that's the line he handed them."

"What did he tell them?"

"Told them that Fritch had a tape recording that contained evidence in a case that might be filed against Ned Bain, that you were negotiating to buy that evidence."

Mason's face darkened.

"Brogan said that something went wrong with the dictating machine when he was playing the record for you yesterday, that you had insisted on a replay of the tape in order to be certain that Brogan could deliver the merchandise if your client could pay the price, that Brogan told you it was only something wrong with the machine, that actually you had managed to slip one over on him, that you had gummed up the works in some way.

"Brogan told Holcomb that he's satisfied you managed in some way to polarize the recording tape so that anything that was on it completely disappeared. He thinks that you listened to the tape once in order to find out what was on it, then worked your hocus-pocus so that the tape went blank.

"He told Holcomb that he reported all this to Fritch, that Fritch at first seemed very much concerned and then said that it would be all right, that Brogan should make an appointment for nine o'clock in the morning, that some time during the night Fritch would dig up a duplicate original of the tape recording."

"How?" Mason asked.

"Brogan claimed he didn't know."

"Innocent, isn't he?"

"Of course, Brogan is trying to claim that it wasn't blackmail. He also says that this is the first he knew that the tape recording he had wasn't the original tape recording, that he now realizes, of course, that it must have been a dubbed copy and Fritch was holding some sort of an original spool of tape."

"Have they found that spool?"

"They've torn Fritch's apartment to pieces. They can't find a damn thing. They can find lots of blank tape and quite a few machines for playing and recording, but that's all."

Mason frowned. "Then if Fritch had a master spool some place, it's disappeared."

"It's disappeared. Is *your* nose clean in this thing, Perry?"

Mason grinned.

"I'm simply telling you," Drake said, "not because I want to pry into your business, but because I think they've got something on you."

"I'm playing them close to my chest," Mason admitted.

"Well, keep playing them close to your chest, Perry. Don't for heaven's sake, make any statement that is contrary to fact because I think Holcomb has laid a trap and I'm afraid you've already walked into it."

"Then I'll have to walk right out again."

"It may not be that simple. Is Della in the clear?"

"I think so. I told her to go out to the Bain place. I want to find out about things out there before Sergeant Holcomb starts sweating the family."

"Well," Drake said, "you may have something there. Holcomb isn't working on that angle at the moment. He seems to be getting some dope on you. Right at the moment he's giving Brogan the works."

"He should," Mason said dryly.

"He's doing that all right, and Brogan is sweating blood. And, of course, they're going through the Fritch apartment, the one he rented under the name of Reedy. Did you know that the guy was all prepared for a regular siege? He could hole up in that apartment and just never go out."

Mason raised his eyebrows.

"He had enough food in there to last him for a year," Drake went on. "Frozen food that would keep him living like a king. He had everything for a balanced diet. Meat, potatoes, fruits, vegetables, ice cream, frozen biscuits, flour, bacon, eggs, butter. In short, everything a guy could possibly want. Now here's something, Perry. I can't get the low-down on it, but the police have been finding fingerprints out there in Brogan's apartment. They're not Fritch's fingerprints. They're not Brogan's fingerprints. Someone has been in there and has been going through things."

"The deuce," Mason said.

Drake looked at him sharply. "You wouldn't have been dumb enough to have left any fingerprints, would you, Perry?"

"I tell you I didn't go in there," Mason said. "I was in there yesterday, however."

"Of course, the prints may have been made yesterday," Drake said. "But they *could* have been made when the murder was committed."

Mason frowned thoughtfully.

Abruptly his telephone shrilled, breaking the silence.

Mason grabbed for the phone. "Excuse me, Paul. That's the unlisted number. Only you and Della Street have that. Hello."

Mason heard Della Street's voice, sharp-edged with excitement.

"Chief, you'd better jump in your car and get out here just as fast as you can."

"Where?"

"The Bains'."

"What's happened?"

"Ned Bain."

"What about him?"

"Dead," she said, "and there are some things I think you should know about before Sergeant Holcomb gets here."

"Good Lord," Mason said, "it isn't a case for Holcomb, is it?"

"No. It's a natural death—in a way," Della Street told him, "but his death *could* have been tied in—in a way."

Mason said, "I'll be right out. Wait for me."

He slammed down the telephone, said to Drake, "Don't get more than two feet away from a phone, Paul. I may need something in a hurry. I'm on my way."

"Where?"

"Bains'."

"Is there another corpse out there?"

Mason nodded. "This one is a natural death."

"Try telling that to Holcomb."

"I'm going to try telling nothing to Holcomb. Find out everything you can about Fritch and Brogan. Put as many men on the job as you have to. Get busy. I'm on my way."

Mason grabbed his hat, dashed out through the exit door of his private office, sprinted for the elevator, jabbed at the down button, and when he had entered the cage said to the operator, "Can you shoot it all the way down? This is an emergency."

"Yes, Mr. Mason," the girl said, and threw the control over, dropping the cage to the ground floor. Two or three other passengers looked at Mason curiously as the lawyer dashed into the lobby and made a run for the parking lot where he kept his car.

Fifteen minutes later Mason was running up the cement walk to the old-fashioned, gingerbread-studded porch of the Bain house.

Della Street, who had been waiting for him, opened the door and said, "Come on in, Chief. The doctor's here."

"What doctor is it, Della?"

"Dr. Flasher. He's the one who had been treating Mr. Bain. Here he is now."

Sylvia Atwood showed up with a tall, tired-looking man in his middle fifties, who peered at Mason from under bushy eyebrows. Suddenly his face lit up. "Well, well," he said, "Mr. Mason. They told me they'd sent for you."

"This is Dr. Flasher, Mr. Mason," Sylvia said.

Mason and the doctor shook hands.

"And this is my brother, Jarrett Bain."

A tall, heavy, slow-moving man peered at Mason through thick-lensed spectacles, took the lawyer's hand and squeezed it with powerful fingers. "Glad to know you, Mr. Mason."

Mason said, "This is a surprise. I thought you were prowling around in the ruins at Yucatan."

"I was. I got Sis's telephone call and decided I'd better be here. Luckily I managed to pick up a cancellation and came right through."

Mason said, "You made a quick trip. When did you get here?"

"This morning," Sylvia Atwood interposed quickly.

"I haven't had a chance to talk with you, Sylvia," Jarrett said. "I guess you're still relying on my wire. I got here—"

Mason looked at his watch. "Tell me about Mr. Bain," he said to Dr. Flasher, trying to appear unhurried, yet conscious of every passing second.

"There's not much to tell, Mr. Mason. The heart muscle was seriously impaired. The only thing that I could do was to prescribe absolute, complete rest, hoping that the heart muscle might pick up again, but the muscle had pretty much lost its tone. Excitement would have proven fatal, and—well, after all, Mr. Mason, the man has gone, so there's no use second-guessing."

Sylvia Atwood interposed quickly, "Dr. Flasher is trying to tell you that death was quite normal and was rather to have been expected. Dr. Flasher is going to sign a death certificate so there won't be any necessity for a lot of red tape."

"You've established the cause of death?" Mason asked.

"Yes, yes, certainly," Dr. Flasher said. "It was simply that a tired heart muscle couldn't carry the load any longer. We all have to go some time. Mr. Bain had had a focal infection which didn't do his condition any good. If I could have caught that a few years earlier things might have been a lot better, but—well, that's the way it is, particularly with these men who have had an outdoor background. They think they're rugged, tough and indestructible. Perhaps they might be if they'd only continue living outdoors. But experience teaches us that an outdoor man seriously jeopardizes his health when he decides to alter his mode of living and remain within four walls."

Mason turned to Sylvia Atwood. "I hope this discussion isn't hurting you too much," he said. "I'm not asking questions simply because of idle curiosity."

"I understand," she said. "I shall miss Dad terribly. I'm shocked, of course, and I have a great sense of loss, but it hadn't been unexpected. I understand your interest, Mr. Mason."

"Apparently he died quietly and without pain," Dr. Flasher interposed. "There was a telephone by the side of his bed. There's no indication that he even made any motion toward it. He died quietly, probably in his sleep."

"Well, that's a relief," Sylvia Atwood said.

Dr. Flasher, keeping his eyes on Perry Mason, went on, "I've been very much interested in following your career, Mr. Mason. I hardly expected to meet you here, although Mrs. Atwood told me that she had consulted you. You will, I suppose, have charge of the legal details in connection with the estate."

"I think," Mason said, "it's a little early to discuss that as yet, but I came out here as soon as I learned what had happened. I have met Mr. Bain and I am handling some business for the family."

"Yes, yes. Well, I must be getting on. I'm terribly sorry about what happened, but it couldn't have been avoided. If I had been here right at the moment, I might—I just *might* have prolonged life for a little while, but I think frankly it's better this way. I don't think your father knew what happened, Mrs. Atwood. I think he simply slipped off in his sleep. It's rather a surprise too, because when I saw him yesterday I felt that there had been some definite improvement. Of course, at his age and with his history you can't expect a heart muscle to be completely rejuvenated, but there had been very satisfactory progress. As a matter of fact, I was very much surprised at the news when you telephoned."

"When did he pass away, doctor?"

"I would say some time early this morning, perhaps five or six o'clock. It isn't particularly important to determine the exact time in a case of this sort."

"No, I suppose not. Tell me, there won't be any postmortem, will there?"

"Oh, I hope not!" Sylvia exclaimed.

"No, no, no, don't worry about that, my dear. It's perfectly natural. I'll sign a death certificate. You can notify the mortician, or would you prefer to have me do it?"

"Do you know someone who is good and dependable?" Sylvia asked.

"Yes, yes, of course, my dear. I'll be glad to do it for you."

"I think that would be the better way," Sylvia said. "Don't you, Jarrett?"

They paused, looking toward Jarrett Bain, waiting for his answer.

Jarrett, a vague, indefinite smile on his face, stood there with his arms folded, looking down at them, saying nothing.

"Don't you think so, Jarrett?" Sylvia asked.

"Eh, how's that? I beg your pardon."

"That Dr. Flasher should arrange for the mortician."

"Oh, yes, yes, of course."

Sylvia Atwood flashed Mason a glance, said to Dr. Flasher, "This is rather a harrowing experience. I'm worried about Hattie and—"

"It's been a shock to her all right," Dr. Flasher said. "I've given her a hypodermic. I gave her a good dose. I want her to sleep and be undisturbed."

Sylvia nodded quickly. Her eyes flashed another quick glance at Mason, then she was looking at Dr. Flasher earnestly.

"I think," she said, "if we can expedite arrangements just as much as possible it will help. If you can explain to the mortician that while this death wasn't unexpected it has, nevertheless, come at the end of a long battle and that some of the family are quite upset. In other words, rush things as much as possible. I'd like to have the body moved and the embalming done and everything before Hattie wakes up."

Dr. Flasher said, "I know a mortician who will be most considerate. I'll notify him."

"At once?" Sylvia asked.

"Yes, yes, of course. Just as soon as I get back to my office."

"And there won't be any difficulties, any red tape, any formalities?"

"No, absolutely not, my dear. Don't worry about it. You're getting yourself in something of a state. I'll sign a death certificate, the body will be moved, they'll go right ahead with the orderly process of embalming, and you can make arrangements for the funeral services."

Sylvia moved toward his side, took his arm. "You're wonderful, Dr. Flasher, simply wonderful."

Dr. Flasher turned to look back over his shoulder, smiled and waved at Mason, said, "It was a real pleasure, Counselor. I'll see you again."

Mason nodded.

Sylvia Atwood escorted Dr. Flasher to the door. Mason watched her for a moment, then turned to look at the tall archaeologist standing beside him.

"Rather a shock to you," Mason said.

"Eh, how's that?"

"I said it was a shock to you."

"Oh yes, of course. Poor Dad. I wanted him to take life easier some time ago but he was always full of drive. You wonder why.

"After you've been prowling around through ruins erected by people who lived, loved and died a thousand years ago, and see the way the jungle has crept up over their temples, obliterated their market places, destroyed their works of art, smothered their culture, you realize that the individual shouldn't make life a rat race but a dignified and leisurely journey into the field of universal knowledge.

"Well, if you'll excuse me, Mr. Mason, I'll be seeing you."

Jarrett Bain turned and stalked slowly away.

Della Street said in a low voice to Perry Mason, "Gosh, *his* head's in the clouds! Sylvia's putting something over."

"What?" Mason asked.

"I don't know. Here she comes now."

Sylvia, having let Dr. Flasher out of the front door, came hurrying up to Mason. She gripped his arm with fingers that were tight with agitated suspense and trembling a little.

"I *must* see you, Mr. Mason," she said in a low, intense voice.

"You're seeing me," Mason told her.

The green eyes flashed quickly at Della Street, then away.

"There won't be any delay, any post-mortem, any red tape?" she asked.

"Not if Dr. Flasher signs the death certificate, not unless someone in authority interposes an official question."

"That police sergeant can be very, very disagreeable."

Mason nodded.

"He might—well, of cours. . . ."

Mason said, "You wanted to see me about something. Get it off your chest."

She looked around her to make certain no one was in a position to overhear, glanced once more at Della Street, then said under her breath, "Dad did it."

"Did what?" Mason asked.

"Killed J.J."

"What?" Mason exclaimed.

She nodded.

"Look here," Mason said, "let's get this straight. Your father was home in bed. Fritch was killed apparently between midnight and three o'clock this morning and—"

"Mr. Mason," she said, "Dad did it. I *know* that. I can prove it if I have to. I don't want to be the one to do it. But you must remember that's the fact and I don't think we should try to conceal it. I'm afraid we'll get in trouble if we do try to conceal it."

"Well," Mason said dryly, "you hardly wish to be placed in the position of discovering your father's death and then babbling to the authorities he murdered the man whose corpse you found this morning."

"No one knows I found it," she said quickly, sharply. "I stuck by the story that we had all met together there in front of Brogan's apartment. That was the way you wanted it, wasn't it?"

"That was what you told Holcomb?"

"Yes."

"Then," Mason said, "we can't change it very well, can we?"

"No. There's no reason why we should."

"Of course," Mason told her, "you should be doing everything you could legitimately do to protect your father's memory and—"

"Listen, Mr. Mason, you and I are practical people. Now I'm telling you I may not have a chance to talk to you again for some little time."

"Why?"

She said, "Don't be stupid, Mr. Mason. I'm going to be prostrated with grief and I can't discuss these things in the presence of other people. They don't know what we know. And, of course, none of this can come from me without making it appear that I'm an undutiful daughter, but Dad brooded over what you had told him about Fritch and Brogan. He couldn't sleep. Last night about twenty minutes past twelve he got up and took the car. He wasn't supposed to drive. He wasn't even supposed to go out. He wasn't supposed to have any excitement, but he had been taking medicine that made him feel better and he was strong enough to do what he felt had to be done."

"And what was that?" Mason asked.

"He went up to face J.J., to call him a liar and a scoundrel, and demand that record."

"What record? The one that Brogan had?"

"No, no, please don't be so difficult, Mr. Mason. The one you told Dad that Fritch had, the master record, the one that had been spliced."

"Go on," Mason said.

"He and Fritch had an argument. I suppose Dad lost his temper. No one will ever know what happened now, but I know Dad was up there. Dad got back here around half-past one or two this morning. He parked the car and went in to bed.

"Apparently the strain he had put on his heart had been too much. There had been excitement and—well, you wonder why Dad didn't die right there in his tracks, but somehow he managed to carry through and get back here."

"Go on," Mason said, making no effort to conceal his skepticism.

"That's what happened," she said. "Dad killed him. I can't be the one to let the authorities realize that, but somehow, Mr. Mason, you must see that they do understand it."

"*I* must?"

"Yes, someone has to."

"Why not let them find out for themselves?" Mason asked.

"They might not find out and they might—well, they might try to pin it on someone else."

"You, for instance?" Mason asked.

"Possibly."

"Your father," Mason said, "is dead. He's not here to defend himself. He can't speak for himself. How do you know that he went out last night between twelve and three?"

"It was about twenty minutes past twelve. I know because I followed him."

"You did?"

"Yes."

"Where?"

"To that apartment house."

"Why didn't you stop him?"

"I—I thought for a while that I would, and then I thought it might be better for Dad to get it off his chest and handle it in his own way. To tell you the truth, Mr. Mason, I wasn't certain, I couldn't be certain, that—that *hadn't* been some association between Dad and J.J.

"Even if you are correct about that recording and even if J.J. had faked it, there still *could* have been something, some previous tie-up between him and Dad. Oh, I tell you, I did a lot of thinking, but I finally decided to let Dad go ahead and handle it his own way."

"Did anyone else see your father leave?" Mason asked.

She shook her head.

"I'm afraid," Mason said coldly, "there would have to be some other proof, something that—"

She moved close to him. "Mr. Mason," she said, "I have the proof."

"What?"

"I have the *proof.*"

"Go on," Mason said.

She said, "A few minutes before Dr. Flasher came I went in to say my own private last farewell to Dad. I put my hand under the pillow of his bed to straighten it out a little bit, to straighten out his head."

"Go on," Mason said. "What happened?"

"There was something under the pillow."

"What?"

"The spool of tape."

"Are you telling me the truth?" Mason exclaimed.

"Of course I am. It was the spool of tape, the original recording that Fritch had. It's spliced where it had been put together just like you said it would be. Dad had got hold of it in some way. He carried it back with him and put it under his pillow. It was there."

"What did you do with it?"

She said, "I put it in a safe place—that is, the only place where it's safe for the moment. I'm going to get it and give it to you, then you must use your own judgment.

"But please, Mr. Mason, please don't misunderstand what I say. Dad has gone. I don't know whether he killed J.J. in self-defense or not. Dad is the one who was responsible for the death of J.J. Fritch. Fritch is dead and Dad is dead. They can't punish him. We *must,* simply must see that somehow the authorities get the lead that will start them investigating Dad. I don't want to be the one that gives them that lead, but if necessary I will break down and tell them."

"Go on," Mason said. "You have that spool of tape. What else?"

"Isn't that enough?"

"Do you have anything else?"

"Why do you ask?"

"Because I want to get the whole story."

"I have—I have the ice pick."

"And where did you get that?"

"This morning, when the body fell out of that liquor closet and rolled right at my feet. It was terrible! Horrible!"

"Never mind that," Mason said. "You can pull the dramatic part later. Where was the ice pick?"

"Still in J.J.'s body."

"Where?"

"In his body."

"I mean what part of his body?"

"The chest."

"What did you do with it?"

"I pulled it out and put it in my purse."

"Why did you do that?"

"Because it was our ice pick."

"How did you know?"

"I could recognize it. Ours is a distinctive ice pick. Edison Doyle gave it to us. He found a place where they were on sale. They're big ice picks with a distinctive metal band around the top so you can use them as a hammer to crush ice if you want."

Mason said, "You talk as if there were more than one."

"Yes, Edison saw them on sale. He bought three. He was laughing about it at the time. He said he was giving us one, was keeping one and was going to save the third as a wedding present for whichever one of us girls got married first."

"And you recognized this ice pick?"

"Yes."

"When you first found the body this morning?"

"Yes. Can't you see, Mr. Mason? At that time I was trying to protect Dad at any cost. I didn't know he'd gone on to a higher court. So, much as I hated to touch the thing, I pulled that ice pick out of the body and put it in my purse. Then I ran to the door and met you and Miss Street."

"And Sergeant Holcomb didn't search your purse?" Mason asked.

"Oh, of course, but I didn't have it then."

"What had you done with it?"

"Put it in the coiled fire hose on the lower floor where no one would think of looking for it, but where I could pick it up again after they'd finished questioning me."

"So," Mason said, "you discovered the body, and you have the murder weapon?"

"That's right. I've hidden it temporarily where no one will look for it, but I wanted to ask you what I should do about it? I—"

Steps sounded behind them. Edison Doyle came rushing up to them.

"Hello, Mr. Mason," he said, and then all in one breath, "Sylvia, what the devil's this?"

"What?" Sylvia asked.

Doyle thrust forward a spool of tape.

"*Where* did you get that?" Sylvia flared.

"From the drawer in Hattie's dresser."

"What were you doing looking in there?"

"At Dr. Flasher's suggestion I was to stay with her until she dropped off to sleep. He gave her a hypo, you know. There were tears on her face and when she dropped off to sleep I looked for a handkerchief. I opened the top drawer in the bureau and this was lying right on top."

"Oh, Edison," Sylvia said, "you—you've done something now—I—I don't know."

"But what *is* it?" Edison Doyle said.

"You shouldn't have found it there," Sylvia Atwood said. "I had found it earlier. It was under Dad's pillow. I put it there until I could ask Mr. Mason about it. Because Hattie had been given a hypo and put to sleep and wasn't to be disturbed I felt certain no one would go in there. I didn't want anyone to know until I could ask Mr. Mason—"

Abruptly she put her hands to her face and started to cry.

"There, there," Doyle said, putting his arm around her shoulders and patting her reassuringly. "It's all right, Sylvia. Mr. Mason is here. He'll tell us what to do. You poor girl, you're all unstrung!"

Her shoulders shook convulsively with sobs.

Della Street wordlessly reached out and took the spool of tape from Edison Doyle's fingers.

As soon as she had done so, Edison Doyle, finding both hands free, promptly and naturally circled Sylvia Atwood with his arms, held the sobbing figure close to him.

"Poor little kid," he said, "you've had more than you can take."

Sylvia sobbed for a moment, then said, "Oh, Edison, you're *such* a comfort! Mr. Mason, will you please take charge of things—of everything?"

"Everything's going to be all right," Edison Doyle went on. "You come with me. You're going to have to lie down and keep quiet."

He gave Mason a significant look, slipped his arm around Sylvia's waist and led her out of the room.

"Well," Della Street said, looking at the spool of tape, "that's that!"

"I think," Mason said, "that we'll see if it is."

"You mean we listen to it?"

"I mean we listen to it."

"And then what?"

"And then," Mason said, "if it turns out to be that master spool of spliced tape we find ourselves in a hell of a fix."

"And if it shouldn't be?"

Mason grinned. "We're in a hell of a fix anyway."

"And," Della Street said bitterly, "not being a woman you can't break out crying on Sergeant Holcomb's shoulder and have him solicitously put you to bed."

"No," Mason said, "but he can solicitously put me out of circulation, and don't ever kid yourself but what he's damned anxious to do just that."

"And the murder weapon?" she asked.

"Fortunately she didn't tell me what she'd done with that. Washed it and put it in the ice box, I suppose."

"Should you find out?"

He shook his head. "Then I'd be an accessory after the fact. This tape recording is evidence, but not of murder. But a murder weapon is something altogether different. We'll let our little green-eyed minx take care of that."

"She won't," Della Street said. "She's too busy stealing her sister's boyfriend."

"No, she's just giving her sex appeal its morning exercise," Mason said.

"That's what *you* think. Come on, Chief, if we're going to listen to that tape recording let's do it before there are any more murders."

"More murders? How many do you think there have been already?"

"*I* count two to date," she said.

CHAPTER 9

Mason escorted Della Street to the place where their cars were parked.

"Take your car, Della," Mason said, "and follow me to the office."

He helped her into her car, closed the door.

"Chief, let me take it."

"What?"

"The spool of tape recording."

Mason shook his head.

"They wouldn't search me."

"You forget," Mason told her. "You're in this thing too. You were up there at Brogan's apartment this morning."

"Chief, I wish you wouldn't—"

"It's all right, Della," he told her. "There are times when an attorney has to take chances if he's going to represent his client."

"Who's your client?" she asked sharply.

"Technically, I suppose it's Sylvia Atwood, but actually I think we're representing the cause of justice."

"Well," Della Street said, "personally I don't think they're the same."

"Perhaps they aren't," he conceded. "We'll try to find out. Meet me at the office. Try not to get pinched for speeding. I'm going fast."

"I'll be right on your tail," she told him.

Mason jumped in his car, started the motor, pushed it into speed. From time to time he looked in his rearview mirror. Each time he looked Della Street was pounding along right behind him.

Mason swung his car into the parking space at the office and Della Street parked her car directly beside his.

Mason walked over to join her. "Okay, Della, we've made it so far."

"So far, so good," she said.

They went up in the elevator in silence, walked down the corridor to Mason's private office.

Della Street opened the door with her latchkey. Mason entered the office. Once inside they moved with the silence of conspirators. Della Street pulled a tape recorder from the closet, connected it up, turned it on and motioned to Perry Mason for the spool of recorded tape.

Mason handed it to her. Della Street put it on the tape recorder, ran the free end of the tape through the recording head, put it on the take-up spool, glanced at Mason.

Mason nodded, said, "Keep the volume down, Della."

Della Street turned the volume down low, started the machine on playback.

There was a moment of silence, then a few sounds of electrical static. Suddenly the voice of J.J. Fritch came out of the loudspeaker.

Della Street immediately turned down the volume another notch.

In silence they sat listening to the conversation between the two men who were now dead, the voices startlingly life-like.

After some five minutes Mason said, "Okay, Della, switch it off. There's no question but what this is it. Also there's no question in my mind but what it's a fake recording."

"Yes, you can hear the difference in some of those questions, the ones that have been spliced in when J.J. Fritch went to a sound studio and—"

The door from Mason's outer office opened.

"I'm not seeing anyone, Gertie," Mason called out sharply.

The door continued to open.

Della Street jumped to her feet. She gave an expression of annoyance and started toward the door.

The door swung all the way open. Lt. Arthur Tragg of the Homicide Squad stood on the threshold.

"Hello, Perry," he said. "Hello, Miss Street."

"You!" Mason said.

Della Street promptly pulled the plug which shut off the current from the tape recording machine, wound up the connecting wire and started to put on the cover.

"Leave it," Tragg said.

"How come?" Mason asked.

"As it happens," Tragg said, "I have a search warrant."

"A search warrant?"

Tragg nodded.

"For what?"

"This office."

"And what the devil do you expect to find in this office?" Mason asked.

Tragg said, "I'm sorry, Mason, I hate to do this to you. I came myself instead of letting Holcomb come because I didn't want any trouble and I was afraid Holcomb might rub it in."

"What's the occasion of the search warrant?"

Tragg said, "I am searching for a certain master spool of spliced tape which was stolen from the apartment of J.J. Fritch this morning.

"I have a couple of my men in the outer office keeping your receptionist occupied. She felt certain you weren't in so she didn't try to ring the phone and tip you off."

"We just came back," Mason said. "I hadn't reported to her that we were in the office."

"So I gathered," Tragg said. "I started in here armed with my search warrant, got as far as the door, heard the sound of a tape recording being played back, so I eased the door open a crack and listened. Now if you don't mind I'll take that spool of tape into custody as evidence."

"Evidence of what?" Mason asked.

"Evidence of motive in the murder of J.J. Fritch. And if you can keep your shirt on, Perry, I'm going to take a chance and tip you off to some valuable information."

"What?" Mason asked.

"I'm sticking my neck out," Tragg said. "I shouldn't do it."

Mason started to say something, then, at the expression he saw on Tragg's face, held his comment.

"Go ahead," he invited.

Tragg said, "You are in a spot."

"I've heard that before," Mason told him.

"You've been in spots before and got out of them. This time you're going to have a job getting out."

"Go on," Mason said.

Tragg said, "Your client, Sylvia Atwood, got to George Brogan's apartment this morning right around eight-forty to keep a nine o'clock appointment. She was twenty minutes early. She went in and did a lot of prowling."

"And that puts *me* in a spot?" Mason asked.

Tragg grinned. "You haven't heard me out yet."

"Go ahead," Mason said. "Let's hear the rest of it."

"Sylvia Atwood," Tragg went on, "entered that apartment around eight-forty. She was in there searching for a spool of tape that was purported to have a conversation between her father and J.J. Fritch on it, the spool of recorded tape that you and Miss Street were just listening to on your machine."

"Go on," Mason said, "we're listening."

"Sylvia Atwood will eventually admit," Lt. Tragg went on, "that at about nine o'clock she came to the liquor closet. She opened the door, and then gave a terrific scream, turned and ran in panic to confront you and Della Street at the door of Brogan's apartment."

"How very, very interesting," Mason said. "I suppose you're going to claim that after having been in there for twenty minutes she suddenly discovered the body of J.J. Fritch?"

"No, I'm not," Tragg said. "That's just the point. *She* is."

"Go on," Mason said.

"The point is that she knew you and Della Street would be there at the door of the apartment at about nine o'clock. She waited until she heard you outside the door, then she moved to the liquor closet, climbed up on a chair, jumped to the floor so as to give a jar, let out a terrific scream, turned and ran toward the door."

Mason said, "I'm listening, Tragg."

"And then," Tragg went on, "she told you and Miss Street that the body of J.J. Fritch was in there, and you told her to stand at the door with Della Street, reading the note that Brogan had left on the door for you, pretending that you had just come to the place.

"You told them that you were going into Fritch's apartment and search for a master tape recording, that there was about one chance in a hundred you might find it, that as soon as Brogan showed up Sylvia Atwood was to press the bell button on Fritch's apartment twice.

"As soon as you heard that signal you were going to come to the door of Fritch's apartment. You would wait until the two young women and Brogan had entered Brogan's apartment, and then you'd come along treading on their heels, pretending that you'd been parking the car."

Mason's eyes narrowed.

"Well?" Tragg said.

"I suppose," Mason said, "from all of the detail with which you are giving this conversation, you must have heard it from the lips of some witness?"

"That's right," Tragg said, "although I'd probably be disciplined if anybody knew I'd told you."

"And, under the circumstances, the witness could be none other than Sylvia Atwood. Since she's my client I won't comment on her veracity or the motives which might have prompted her."

"You're wrong," Tragg said.

"Wrong in what?"

"Wrong in guessing the identity of the witness who told us this, who related the conversation."

"Well, who *was* the witness?" Mason asked.

"Perry Mason."

"Oh, I see. Talking in my sleep again, eh?" Mason observed jocularly.

"No," Tragg said, "you'll have to think a long while before you get the answer, Perry."

"What's the answer?"

"Brogan had laid a trap for you. He wanted to find out what you and Mrs. Atwood really felt about the evidence he had, about whether you were planning to pay off, or whether you were going to fight. So he arranged to be in a poker game which would keep him out all night. He left his apartment door unlocked and left a note on it for you stating that if he happened to be a few minutes late you were to go on in and sit down.

"And then he installed a tape recorder with a microphone so ingeniously placed that it would pick up sounds from within the apartment and sounds on the outside of the door in the corridor. He plugged in an electric clock of the type used to turn on radio or television sets and set the time control at eight-fifty.

"You'd be surprised to find how clearly the sounds of Sylvia Atwood jumping on the floor, her scream and the subsequent conversation among the three of you come in on that tape recording.

"George Brogan broke down under Sergeant Holcomb's questioning and told Holcomb the whole business, and gave him the tape."

"I see," Mason said. "My answer is, 'no comment.'"

"I thought that would be your answer," Tragg said. "As a matter of fact I like you, Mason. I think your methods are too damn unconventional. I think you go too far to protect your clients. I think you've skirted the edge of the penitentiary before, and I don't like to see you do it again. I'm telling you this as a friendly tip-off so you won't make a statement that is at variance with the facts of the case. Remember those facts can be established by the sound of your own voice, the sound of Della Street's voice and Sylvia Atwood's voice."

"Thanks," Mason said dryly.

"No thanks at all," Tragg told him. "Now, under the authority of this search warrant, *I'm* going to take that spool of tape recording which you were clever enough to find in the Fritch apartment."

"Suppose I didn't find it there?" Mason said.

Tragg grinned. "Don't be silly, Perry. In view of Brogan's tape recording stating that you were going in there to look for that specific piece of property, you stand a fat chance denying how you happened to acquire it. As a matter of fact, it was on the strength of Brogan's tape recording that I was able to get an order to search your office.

"Quite naturally the judge who issued the search warrant wasn't particularly keen about it. It wasn't until after he'd listened to the tape recording that he rather reluctantly issued the warrant.

"I decided to serve it myself because I was afraid Holcomb would be so keen on trapping you that he might goad you into making some statement that would prove embarrassing later, when you were confronted with that tape recording."

Mason got up from behind his desk, hesitated a moment, walked over and shook hands with Lieutenant Tragg.

"Now then," Tragg said, "I'll take the tape recording."

"Go ahead," Mason told him. "And incidentally, Tragg, while you're about it, check the whereabouts of George Brogan every minute of the time last night."

"Don't worry," Tragg said, "that's been done."

"He has an alibi?"

"Ironbound, copper-riveted, a lead-pipe cinch. He was playing poker with seven men. One of them happens to be a friend of the Chief of Police."

"What time did the game start?"

"About ten o'clock and it lasted until Brogan broke away this morning about eight-fifteen, stating he had an important appointment, that he was going to have to hurry to get a cup of coffee and a little breakfast, that he wouldn't have time to clean up. He'd been trying to break away ever since seven o'clock, but he was winning and they kept holding him on for one more round."

"He was there all the time?"

"He was out of the game about thirty minutes around five o'clock in the morning," Tragg said. "He had a losing streak, had dropped all of the money he had, and went out to call on a friend to get some cash. He returned at about five-thirty with fifteen hundred dollars. The murder was committed between midnight and three o'clock this morning."

"You're certain?" Mason asked.

"Thanks for the buggy ride," Mason told him.

"Not at all," Tragg said.

He took the spool of tape recording, scribbled a receipt to Mason, turned and left the office.

Della Street looked at Mason with wide eyes.

Mason shrugged his shoulders.

"Chief, can't you tell them—shouldn't you tell them where you *really* got that tape recording?"

"Not yet," Mason said.

"Later on no one will believe you."

"They won't believe me now."

"But, Chief, Sylvia can't help you if you wait to tell your story. They'll think it's something you've hatched up between you. You should protect yourself now by telling the whole truth and calling on Sylvia and Edison Doyle and—"

"We tell the police nothing," Mason interrupted. "This is a law office, not an information bureau."

"It will get you in bad," she said.

"Then I'll have to be in bad. I've been in bad before, and I probably will be in bad again."

"What do we do?"

Mason motioned toward the telephone. "Get Sylvia Atwood on the line. Tell her to get up here just as fast as she can make it."

CHAPTER 10

Sylvia Atwood sat in the client's chair in Mason's office. Her eyes were fixed steadily on the lawyer now. There were no more flickering glances. She was regarding him as cautiously as a poker player appraises someone who has just shoved a stack of blue chips into the pot.

"Go ahead," she said.

"That's all of it," Mason said. "We were playing the tape recording to make sure what it was and Tragg walked in with a search warrant."

"So the police have it now?"

"That's right."

"Mr. Mason, you should have done as I told you."

"What?"

"Told them that my father got that tape recording, that he—that he is responsible for what happened up there in the apartment."

"The death of J.J. Fritch?"

"Yes."

"I couldn't tell them that," Mason said.

"Why not?"

"Because I don't know that he was."

"Well you know it now."

"No, I don't. That's why I asked you to come here. I want to know *exactly* what happened. I want to get the *complete* details. You tell me exactly what happened and be careful what you say. Della Street is going to take notes and, in addition to that, I'm going to have a tape recorder taking down everything you say."

"I'm your client," she flared at him. "You've no right to treat me as though I were an adverse party—a suspect."

"You're a client," Mason admitted, "and you also may be a suspect. Now start talking."

Her eyes flashed for a moment, then she said, "Very well, I'll tell you the facts, the true facts, and I'll tell you all of them."

"Go ahead."

She said, "After your conversation with Dad yesterday afternoon he was very upset."

"Naturally," Mason said, "but you must remember that the thing that upset him was not my conversation but what J.J. Fritch had told him."

"Please don't misunderstand me, Mr. Mason. I'm not blaming you. Actually *your* conversation with him quieted his nerves and helped him a lot, but I'm simply trying to fix it from the standpoint of time. It was after you had left yesterday afternoon that we realized Dad was in such a terribly nervous state."

"Go ahead."

"We tried to reach Dr. Flasher and couldn't. He was out on an emergency case, but he had left medicine for Dad and we gave him some of that medicine. It was medicine that was supposed to quiet him and do something to make it easier for the heart to work."

"All right," Mason said. "Then what happened?"

"Dad was nervous. He didn't want to sleep. We sat in the room with him. He dozed from time to time. He didn't think he was sleeping at all. Sometimes he dozed as much as half an hour. By ten o'clock he had quieted down a lot."

"Go ahead," Mason said.

"Edison Doyle had been there earlier in the evening. He, of course, knew all about what was happening. We talked it over and decided we'd take turns keeping an eye on Dad. We thought he might—well, we thought he might take a turn for the worse and might want somebody there on the job."

Mason nodded.

"Edison had some sketches that he had promised against a deadline. They simply had to be out this morning. He said that he'd go up to his office and work until a little after midnight, that he'd come out then and be in a position to take over."

Again Mason nodded.

"We had it agreed that Hattie was to go to bed and get some sleep, that I'd sit up until Dad went to sleep, that then I'd get a couple of hours' sleep. We left a key to the back door under the mat so Edison could come in whenever he got through with his work. He felt that would be one or two o'clock in the morning.

"He was to tiptoe up to one of the guest rooms and go to sleep. I was to fix my alarm clock so I could look in on Dad every hour and a half. If he was sleeping I wouldn't call the others. If he became restless I'd call Edison and let him keep a steady watch for two hours, then I'd watch for two hours.

"We agreed Hattie needed all the sleep she could get. She was right on the ragged edge. We weren't going to call her unless we had to. We got her to agree to take a sleeping pill."

"What happened?" Mason asked. "Go ahead."

"Hattie went to bed. The house quieted down. Everything was perfectly quiet. I looked in on Dad. He seemed to be asleep. I checked to see that the house was locked up, before heading for bed. Then I heard a car being started in the garage. Whoever was driving it was driving very carefully so that it wouldn't disturb anyone. The car came out with the lights off."

"What did you do?"

"I ran to the window. I saw Dad in the car."

"You're sure?"

"Just as sure as I can be, but I verified it."

"How?"

"I ran into his room. He wasn't in the bed. The covers had been thrown back."

"So what did you do?"

"I followed. I dashed out to where I'd left my car parked at the curb, jumped in and followed the car ahead."

"Why didn't you stop him?"

"I don't know why I didn't, Mr. Mason, but I wanted to find out what it was he had in mind, and—well, I guess I was terribly curious. I knew that Dad wouldn't have gone out except on some matter of the greatest emergency, something that was life and death, and I wanted to find out what it was and where he was going."

"Where did he go?"

"I've already told you. He went directly to that apartment house."

"What did you do?"

"I waited, thinking that he'd come out within a few minutes. After about half an hour or so, when he didn't come out, I became very worried and entered the apartment house."

"Then what?"

"You know it's one of those apartment houses where the outer door is always open. There's no one on duty on the inside. You go right up to the apartments without being announced."

"Go on," Mason said.

"The outer door is supposed to be kept latched, but all you have to do is push against it hard and it opens."

"I know," Mason said. "Tell me what you did."

"I went in and started for the elevator. I saw that it was on the floor where Brogan had his apartment. I felt certain Dad was up there. I was just about to press the button for the elevator when I heard the elevator coming down."

"What did you do?"

"I ran for the stairs and ran part way up the first flight of stairs."

"What happened?"

"I heard someone get out of the elevator. I realized, of course, that it probably was Dad. I ran back down the stairs and was able to glimpse the figure just as it went out. The figure was silhouetted against the door. It wasn't Dad, at least I didn't think it was at the time. I thought it was a woman."

"Go on."

"So I took the elevator back up, walked down the corridor and stood fairly near the door of Brogan's apartment, listening. I couldn't hear any voices. I went back to the end of the corridor and waited. When I'd been waiting for about half an hour or so I again walked back down to the apartment. I was good and worried then. This time I went closer and saw there was a note on the door. I looked at the envelope and saw it was addressed to you. I pulled it off, read the note, realized the apartment was unlocked. I put the note back on the door, trying to push the thumb tack into the same hole that it had occupied, but the light wasn't good and I'm not certain I did it."

"Go on."

"I tried the door of the apartment. It was unlocked. I just wanted to find out if Dad was in there. I opened the door and stepped in."

"Go on," Mason said.

"A light was on in the living room. There was no one in there."

"What did you do?"

"I went through the apartment, switching on lights, looking for Dad. He wasn't there."

"Where was J.J. Fritch?"

"At the time, I don't know."

"He wasn't there then?"

"Of course he was, but I didn't know it. His body must have been in the liquor closet, Mr. Mason."

"You didn't open that door?"

"Not then, no."

"So what did you do?"

"At first I felt Dad must be in J.J.'s apartment across the hall. I tried that door. It was locked. I listened. There was no sound, no voices, no noise of any sort.

"I started to ring, then started to wonder if my eyes could have deceived me and if it had really been Dad who had gone out of the door of that apartment house.

"So I went back down to the street and sure enough our car was gone. So then I hurried back home. Dad was in bed, sound asleep, so I went up to bed and went to sleep myself, setting my alarm so I could look in on Dad every hour and a half until seven-thirty.

"Then I dressed, jumped in my car, drove to a restaurant, had breakfast and went to George Brogan's apartment for my appointment with you. Only, knowing that I'd probably find the apartment unlocked, I went about twenty minutes early."

"Then you didn't see anyone after you got back to the house?"

"No. Edison had gone to bed. Jarrett got in on a plane at four o'clock this morning, rented one of those cars you drive yourself so he'd have his own transportation, and let himself in and went to bed."

"You haven't said anything to anyone else about this?"

"Not so far, but I'm going to."

"Why?"

"Because it's the only fair thing to do, Mr. Mason. If Fritch was killed when the police say he was, that was at the time Dad was up in that apartment house.

"Please understand me, Mr. Mason, as long as Dad was alive I did everything I could to protect him, even going to the extent of taking that murder weapon out of the body. Think of the spot I'd have been in if that horrid Sergeant Holcomb had caught me with that ice pick."

"I've been thinking about that," Mason said.

"Well, I cheerfully took all that risk to protect Dad, but now that he's gone we'd be terribly foolish to run risks trying to conceal the facts. Why, they might even try to pin the murder on one of *us!*"

Mason frowned deeply as he gave the problem his full attention.

"Don't you see, Mr. Mason," she went on, "Dad is dead. He can't be punished. I am willing to assume that he acted in self-defense, but I am not willing to try to protect his memory by concealing essential facts."

"You haven't told Sergeant Holcomb anything about this?"

"Not yet. Of course, at first I didn't have any proof. Later on I found that tape recording under Dad's pillow."

"And what did you do with it?"

"I thought I'd conceal it some place where no one would look until I could ask you about it. I was in something of a panic."

"Go ahead," Mason said.

"I knew that Dr. Flasher had given Hattie a hypo, told her to undress and get into bed. I slipped into her room pretending I wanted to make sure she was all right. She was undressing. I hid the tape recording in the top dresser drawer where she keeps her handkerchiefs. I felt that no one would look in there because they wouldn't want to disturb Hattie."

"Then what?"

"Well, Hattie was still nervous even after the hypo. Dr. Flasher thought it would be a good thing for Edison to go in and sit by the bed and talk with her. He said to talk quietly, in a low, even voice, talking about things that weren't connected with Dad's death, using long sentences and using a monotone as much as possible. He thought that would help her go to sleep.

"You know the rest."

Mason said, "Brogan had a tape recording made of our conversation in front of the door of his apartment this morning. He's turned that over to the police. They know that you discovered the body. They know that I announced I was going into Fritch's apartment to see if I could find that spool of tape recording."

Sylvia Atwood thought that over for a few minutes. Abruptly she got to her feet. "That settles it," she said. "I've made up my mind what I'm going to do."

"Now wait a minute," Mason said. "You haven't made up your mind to anything. If you want me to represent you, you're going to have to follow my advice."

"But you're not representing me."

"You retained me."

"That was to represent the family, not me. *I'm* not in any trouble, not now—particularly not after what I'm going to do."

"You may think you're not in any trouble," Mason said, "and you may be kidding yourself."

"But I'm not. That's ridiculous. Personally, Mr. Mason, I think you're being altogether too conservative about this thing, and I think you've held your own counsel entirely too long. I think you should have passed the information along to the police."

"What's happened to Hattie?" Mason asked.

"She's still asleep. She'll probably be asleep until midnight or later. Dr. Flasher was particularly anxious that she get a good sleep. She's lost a lot of rest lately and she's terribly nervous."

"Now wait a minute," Mason said. "Let's get a few things straight. I want to know the real truth about that body. What happened when you found it?"

"I told you the truth."

"Tell it again, then."

"I was searching. I wondered if Dad had talked to J.J. in there or in J.J.'s apartment. I felt certain you and Miss Street would arrive before Brogan. And since Brogan had no way of knowing that I would know the apartment was unlocked, he wouldn't have expected me to get there much before nine.

"So I got up there about twenty minutes to nine and I started looking around. Well, frankly, I was searching. That's why I kept my gloves on so I wouldn't leave fingerprints.

"I opened the door of the liquor closet. That is, I turned the knob. As soon as I turned it and the latch clicked the door flew open. The body must have been pressing against the door from the inside.

"It was terrible, horrible. It—"

"Never mind all that. Was the body stiff? Had *rigor mortis* set in?"

"I—I can't be sure. I *think* the arms were held up very rigid—bent at the elbows, but I *think* the legs sprawled. There was a sort of bruise on the back, just above the undershirt. Mr. Mason, no one must ever know about that ice pick being in my possession."

"Where is it now?"

"I'm going to get it. Won't it be better if you don't know some of these things? I'll do what is necessary."

"Now just a moment. Where are you going now?" Mason asked, as Sylvia Atwood picked up her purse and got to her feet.

She started to say something, then changed her mind, looked at him with her eyes wide and innocent.

"Why, home, of course," she said. "That's my place, to be with Hattie."

She hurried to the door.

"Wait a minute," Mason said.

"There isn't time," she retorted, and jerked the door open.

CHAPTER 11

Paul Drake phoned Mason at about three o'clock.

"Hear the latest, Perry?"

"What?"

"From a quote, undisclosed but authentic source, unquote, the police have been advised that Ned Bain got up from his sick bed last night, kept a midnight appointment with J.J. Fritch; presumably murdered him in order to obtain possession of a master tape recording, which Fritch was using in an attempt to blackmail Bain into paying a large sum of money."

"That's been announced to the press?"

"That's right. It just came over the radio in a newscast."

"Who gave them the information?" Mason asked.

"A quote, undisclosed source, unquote. Was that you?"

"No."

"It would be a slick move, making a dead man a murderer. It would get the live ones out from under."

"I didn't do it," Mason said. "Anything else now, Paul?"

"The police recovered the tape recording in question through quote, vigorous, intelligent work, unquote. They ran down a series of clues, decided that the tape recording was in the possession of quote, a prominent downtown lawyer, unquote.

"Police secured a search warrant and entered the office of this lawyer. They found him and his attractive secretary in the lawyer's private office listening to the very tape recording that has become such a valuable piece of evidence in the case."

"The lawyer wasn't named?" Mason asked.

"Wasn't named," Drake said, "but the newscaster announced that his initials were *P. M.*"

"That makes it nice," Mason said. "Thanks for calling."

Mason hung up the telephone, said to Della Street, "Well, the beans are spilled all over the stove. Now we'll have to see what happens."

"She told the police?" Della Street asked.

"The police announced that an undisclosed source of information gave them the tip-off."

"They're investigating?"

Mason nodded.

"Sylvia Atwood might at least have done us the courtesy of telling us what she was going to do," Della Street said.

"Sylvia Atwood," Mason observed, getting up from behind the desk and starting to pace the floor, "is adopting the position that she knows more than her attorney."

"Not *her* attorney," Della Street corrected. "The family attorney."

Mason grinned. "That's right."

He continued pacing the floor.

"This," Della Street said, "will get you off the spot, won't it, Chief?"

"It might if the police believe her."

"Do you think they'll believe her?"

"I would say," Mason said, "that there was only about one chance in ten. They'll think that she's concocting a story in order to get herself out of a jam and get me out of a jam. The public will resent the fact that she was altogether too eager to pin a murder on her dead father before the body was even cold.

"That's going to have the effect of making for very poor public relations, Della."

"I'll say it is," Della Street blazed, "and when they photograph her with those cold eyes of hers, and when it seems she tried to make her dead father the fall guy just as soon as she knew he'd passed away—Gosh, Chief, when you stop to think of it that way it really ties together, doesn't it?"

Mason nodded moodily.

"Of course," Della Street said, "she had the tape recording and—"

"You mean *I* had it."

"Well, she gave it to you."

Mason said, "That's something I'm afraid we can't admit, Della."

"Why not?"

"She's our client."

"But you can at least tell where you got it."

"I can't. Of course, we have Edison Doyle. Presumably he'll tell the police where *he* found it. Police, however, have publicly adopted the position that shrewd detective work enabled them to find the tape recording after I had purloined it from Fritch's apartment.

"If they had to back up on that and if it turned out the tape recording had been given me by someone who had found it, their faces would be red.

"Sergeant Holcomb doesn't like to have his face become red. Tragg will find the facts and face them. Holcomb will move heaven and earth to keep everyone believing I broke into that apartment and purloined that tape."

"And where is that going to leave you?" she asked.

He grinned. "Right behind the eight ball, as usual, but we have to protect our clients, Della, regardless of any other consideration."

"Do you think Brogan really did have the tape recording of what took place in front of his apartment?"

"Sure," Mason said. "Tragg couldn't have repeated that conversation as accurately as he did unless they did have such a tape recording."

The buzzer of the telephone on Della Street's desk sounded.

Mason said, "Tell Gertie I can't see any clients today. Tell her to filter out everything except the important calls. Tell her I'm tied up on an emergency matter of the greatest importance."

Della Street nodded, picked up the telephone, said, "Gertie, Mr. Mason . . . . What. . . . Who. . . . Just a minute."

She turned to Mason.

"Jarrett Bain's out there. He says he simply has to see you, and he seems to be all worked up."

"Is he alone?"

"He's alone."

"I'll see him," Mason said. "Go out and bring him in, Della."

She nodded, hurried through the door to the outer office.

Jarrett Bain, following Della, came striding into Mason's office, his manner radiating indignation.

"Good afternoon, Mr. Bain," Mason said. "Sit down. Tell me what's on your mind."

Bain didn't sit down, but stood towering over Mason's desk, looking down at the lawyer with blazing, angry eyes.

"What's all this about trying to blame the murder of J.J. Fritch on Dad?"

"I don't know," Mason said. "I received a telephone call just a moment ago from the Drake Detective Agency telling me that the police had announced that a quote, undisclosed but authentic source, unquote, had given them a tip-off."

"Wasn't that undisclosed source you?" Bain asked.

Mason shook his head.

Bain glowered at him for a moment, then walked over and sat down in the client's chair as though some of the anger and much of the strength had eased out of him.

"I should have known it," he said, disgustedly.

"Known what?" Mason asked.

"Sylvia," Jarrett said, and there was a world of contempt in his voice.

"You think *she* was the one who told the police?"

"Of course she was," Jarrett said. "She had to do it either through herself or through you. I didn't find out until just an hour or so ago that the tape recording had been found in the drawer of Hattie's dresser. I wish someone had told *me.*

"I guess I'm supposed to be a theorist, Mr. Mason. I'll admit that lots of times I don't keep up with all the gabble-gabble-gabble of conversation that goes on around me, but—my God, if she'd *only* talked with me."

"Just how would that have helped?" Mason asked.

"Why, hang it," Bain said, "Dad didn't go out last night. That's all poppycock."

"How do you know he didn't?"

"Because I was sitting with him," Bain said.

"You were!" Mason exclaimed. "Why, I understood you got home shortly after four this morning and never saw your father alive."

"That was the surmise," Bain said," because no one took the trouble to ask me anything. Sylvia took things for granted and Hattie had been given a hypo."

"You did see him?"

"Of course I saw him. That's what I came home for. Sylvia told me on the long-distance telephone that Dad was in bad shape. She told me that this other matter was pending, and if he got word of it the shock might prove fatal. Of course I came home. What would any son have done under the circumstances?"

"Go ahead," Mason said.

"Well," Jarrett said, "I got home. I had a latchkey and let myself in. Naturally I didn't want to break in on Dad. I looked around to try and find one of the girls."

"Go ahead," Mason said, his eyes narrowed with interest.

"Neither one of the girls was there," Jarrett Bain said. "No one was there. Personally I thought that was a hell of a way to take care of a man who had heart trouble."

Mason exchanged glances with Della Street.

"Go ahead," Mason said, "tell us exactly what you did. Describe your movements in detail if you can."

"Well, that's a big house. It's full of rooms. There are several guest rooms. I lugged my bags up to the first guest room, trying to be as quiet as possible. I saw at once that that was being occupied by Sylvia. She had some things on the dresser. Her overnight bag with her creams and stuff was there, and a nightdress laid out on the foot of the bed.

"So I went on into another guest room and put my things in there. Then I went back downstairs and thought I'd better wake Hattie up and let her know I was home. I knew where she slept.

"I got to the door of her room. It was ajar. I knocked gently. No one said anything. I listened, couldn't hear any breathing, so I went in and switched on the light. Hattie wasn't there."

"Then what did you do?"

"Then I became alarmed about Dad. I tiptoed down the corridor to his room and opened the door just a crack and looked in."

"Your father was there?"

"Dad was there, awake, reading," Jarrett said. "He heard the door, looked up and caught my eye and gave a start of surprise and said, 'Jarrett, what in the world are *you* doing here?'"

"He hadn't expected you?"

"Apparently not," Bain said. "Apparently no one expected me. I had sent a wire stating that I was going to be in on the plane that arrived at four o'clock in the morning, but that wire wasn't delivered until the next morning."

"But you got in *before* four o'clock?" Mason asked.

"Fortunately I was able to catch an earlier plane. By flying from New Orleans to Dallas on a local line I was able to pick up a through plane and got in earlier than would have been the case if I'd waited over in New Orleans and taken the direct plane on which I had reservations."

"Go ahead," Mason said. "What happened?"

"Well, Dad and I talked for a while and—well, I could see Dad was terribly worried. He hadn't been able to sleep much. He said the doctor had given him some medicine to quiet his nerves, but after he'd gone to sleep, he'd wakened and felt pretty jittery. He apparently had no idea he was alone in the house. He said he had a bell that he could ring and one of the girls would bring him anything he needed, but he was doing all right. He had everything right near his hand and he decided to sit up and read a little bit."

"So then what?"

"Well, I knew I shouldn't keep Dad up long, but I sat down and talked with him for about half or three-quarters of an hour. Of course *I* avoided the subject of this blackmail because I didn't think he knew anything about it, but he brought it up himself, told me about Fritch telephoning and threatening him about you coming into the picture and all that."

"Then what?" Mason asked.

"I persuaded Dad to take another one of the capsules that quieted his nerves and told him I'd see him in the morning. He was just as wide awake as could be, but I felt he should try to quiet down, particularly after that capsule I gave him, so I told him *I* was tired and *I* was going to bed."

"Then what?"

"Then I went out and fixed myself a sandwich and a glass of milk in the kitchen, and while I was doing that Edison Doyle showed up."

"You'd met Edison Doyle before?"

"No, I hadn't. I'd been away from home and—well, of course, I'd heard about Edison Doyle and I knew who he was, and that he was interested in Hattie."

"And what happened?"

"Edison Doyle told me that the girls had been a little bit worried about their dad and decided to have someone on duty all night, to look in on him every hour or so. I could see that he assumed I had come home and had taken over the job of watching and that the girls were asleep."

"Did you tell him they weren't home?"

Jarrett shook his head. "No, it wasn't any of his business. I just didn't say anything one way or another."

"And what happened?"

"Well, Edison and I got acquainted and he told me that he'd come up to help watch, that he'd had some work that had to be out that morning, that he'd been up working in the office. His eyes were pretty tired. He'd been straining them over a drawing board making some preliminary sketches and plans. So I told him to go on up and go to bed."

"Where?"

"In the third guest room."

"Did he?"

"That's right. It didn't take much urging."

"Then what?"

"Then," Jarrett said, "after he went to bed, I tiptoed down the corridor, opened the door a crack and looked in on Dad. He had the reading light turned out, just the night light was on and he was sleeping peacefully. I tiptoed back, sat around for a while, began to feel drowsy myself and decided that there was no need having anyone looking in on Dad. I felt certain the girls would be in pretty quick anyway, so I started on up to bed. I decided to set my alarm clock so I could wake up in an hour and a half after I crawled in. I thought I'd just look in on Dad and see how things were going at that time."

"And what happened?"

"Just as I started up the stairs I heard the back door being unlocked. I stood there at the top of the stairs wondering what was happening, and Hattie came in."

"You're sure it was Hattie?"

"Yes."

"How was she dressed?"

"She had on a plaid skirt. I remember that. And she must have been wearing a coat because I'd heard her open the door of the hall closet before she came to where I could see her."

"So what did she do? Did you speak to her?"

"She went to her room. I didn't say a word to her. I'd begun to realize by that time I was plenty tired. I'd been flying on a plane. I'd been up all night. I'd talked with Dad, and I knew Hattie would want to tell me all about how wonderful Edison Doyle was and how happy she was, and how worried she was about Dad, so I decided it could keep. I'm fond of Hattie, but I don't like gushing conversation and all this ga-ga business of young love leaves me cold. Hattie was all right. Anything she had to say could wait until morning."

"So what happened?"

"I went back upstairs. I undressed and took a hot shower. Then just as I'd turned my light off and heaved myself into bed I heard a car door slam out in front of the house. I was curious, so I went to my window and looked out. It was Sylvia's car. She was coming up the sidewalk. Well, I felt everything was under control. I understood that Sylvia was helping out with watching Dad, so I decided I could shut off my alarm clock. So I got into bed and went to sleep."

"How long did you sleep?"

"Pretty long. I didn't get up until around ten in the morning. I was tired."

"And what happened?"

"By that time my wire had been delivered stating that I was arriving on the four o'clock plane. Evidently everyone thought that I'd arrived then and had come on in and had gone to bed."

"But Edison Doyle knew what time you got in."

"Edison Doyle knew that I was there when he arrived, which was around one, I guess, perhaps a little later. But you see, Doyle got up at seven-forty-five and dashed up to his office to meet that client. At least he told me that was what he was going to do.

"Doyle said he was to be there and stand by just in case things got bad. He said Sylvia was able to wake up and then go back to sleep instantly and she'd promised to keep her alarm clock set at intervals, would go down and look in on Dad, then call the others if she felt anyone needed to sit up with him.

"I got up at ten o'clock in the morning, shaved, went downstairs and had some breakfast. I saw Hattie, of course, and had a little talk with her, but she was busy doing chores around the house. I didn't realize it at the time, but I found out afterward that she'd received my wire and had assumed that I came in on the four o'clock plane. She told me Dad was still sleeping. I had some telephoning to do and, as I say, Hattie was busy with housework and getting Dad's breakfast ready. Then along about—I don't know, it must have been nearly eleven, she went in to give Dad his breakfast and that was when she found out he'd passed away.

"Well, of course, after that everything was excitement. We were running around in circles and trying to get Dr. Flasher, and after Dr. Flasher came—I don't know, the house was full of people. You were there, and Miss Street—I don't know exactly when she came. Sylvia had gone out to keep a nine o'clock appointment. She got back in the midst of the excitement. Someone telephoned Edison Doyle and he dashed out. Dr. Flasher gave Hattie a hypodermic and put her to sleep, and—well, that's about it."

Mason nodded.

"Now then," Jarrett said, "I can begin to put two and two together and see what happened. Hattie went out some place. It was pretty cold at that hour of the morning and she may have put on Dad's overcoat. Sylvia may or may not have thought she was following Dad. She might have peeked into his room just as he was in the bathroom, I don't know. But this much I do know—Dad wasn't out of the house, he didn't murder Fritch, and anyone who says he did is a liar."

"What about this tape recording?" Mason asked.

"The one that was supposed to have been under his pillow?"

Mason nodded.

"I don't think it was under his pillow when I was there," Bain said. "It could have been planted there afterward. I don't know. I'll tell you this much, Mr. Mason. Sylvia is a regular little manipulator. She always gets the idea she knows more than anyone else, and she loves to scheme and manipulate things. You give that girl her head and she'll get you into one hell of a mess. Don't say I didn't warn you.

"It never seems to occur to her that someone else may know something. She wants to be little Miss Fix-It and she'll twist and distort and plant false clues and all that trying to have things her way.

"Now I don't know much about law, but I know a lot about Sylvia, and my best guess is that her cute little tendency to manipulate facts and clues could raise merry hell in a murder case.

"Am I right?"

Mason grinned. "You're very, very right."

There was silence for a moment while Mason drummed on his desk, then he said, "Let's try to fix the time as close as we can."

"Well, my plane got in at eleven-forty-five. It took me a few minutes to get my baggage cleared. I had rented a car from a drive-yourself agency. It was waiting for me at the airport. I got home around twelve-thirty."

"Did you look at your watch at any time that you remember?"

"I remember it was around—oh, around one o'clock when I was with Dad. I remember after we'd then been talking a little while I thought he should be getting some sleep, so I put on an act of yawning and talking about being tired."

"How long did you stay after that? I mean in the room with your father."

"Not very long, a few minutes perhaps."

"And then you were in the kitchen eating a sandwich and having a glass of milk when Edison Doyle came in?"

"That's right."

"Edison Doyle had a key?"

"He said Hattie told him the key to the back door would be left under the back doormat. I guess it was. I didn't notice. Anyway, he opened the back door and came in. I remember he locked the door behind him. It's a spring lock, works with a latchkey."

Mason studied the top of his desk in frowning contemplation. He once more began drumming thoughtfully with the tips of his fingers.

"Now then," Jarrett Bain said, "what should we do? It looks as though Sylvia may be trying to confuse the issue. But right now she's certainly started something. Personally I think she has started something she can't finish."

"We have Hattie to consider," Mason said. *"And* Sylvia."

"Don't waste any time worrying about Sylvia," Bain said. "She'll take care of herself. Right now she's managed to put Hattie in something of a spot and has definitely left a great big black mark on

Dad's memory. I like her as a sister, but some of the things she does drive me nuts.

"Now then, she's spread a cockeyed story and as soon as they interview me it'll be established that that story's false."

Mason studied him thoughtfully. "It probably won't occur to them to question you. You may not *have* to be interviewed."

Jarrett Bain shook his head. "No dice, Mr. Mason. I'm sorry but I'm a damn poor liar. Moreover, I have ideas about telling the truth. I have to live with myself."

"You intend to tell your story then?"

"Of course. Anyhow, I have a feeling of loyalty to Dad's memory. I'm doing this much, I'm telling you *first*."

"Where are you going to tell it next?" Mason asked.

"I have an appointment with some guy up at headquarters. Let me see, what's his name now?"

Jarrett took a card out of his pocket, looked at it, said, "A Lieutenant Tragg of Homicide. You know him?"

Mason settled back in his chair and sighed wearily. "I know him."

"Well, I'm on my way up there," Jarrett Bain said, heaving up to his feet. "Didn't realize it was so late. Don't want to keep the guy waiting. Good day, Mr. Mason."

"*Good* day," Mason said as Jarrett walked toward the door.

Silently Mason and Della Street watched the door click shut behind the departing archaeologist.

Della Street sighed in dismay. "The damnedest things happen to us, Chief," she said. "I feel like I want to bawl."

"Who doesn't?" Mason said with a wry grin.

CHAPTER 12

Nervous, almost hysterical knuckles tapped on the hall door of Mason's private office.

Mason glanced at Della Street. "That probably will be Sylvia," he said. "If it is, let her in."

Della Street opened the door a crack, then pulled it all the way open, stood to one side and said, "Come in, Mrs. Atwood."

Sylvia Atwood's eyes showed that she had been crying. She was almost hysterical as she said, "Oh, thank heavens I've found you here, Mr. Mason. Thank heavens. I rang and rang the phone and no one answered—"

"The switchboard is disconnected after the office closes at five," Mason explained.

"They wouldn't give me any other number. They said it was unlisted. Oh, Mr. Mason, I've done the most awful thing, the most terrible thing!"

"All right," Mason said, "tell me just how bad it is."

"I guess I must have been mistaken about one thing, Mr. Mason. It could have been Hattie who went up there to Brogan's apartment. If it was Hattie then she was wearing Dad's overcoat. When that person came down in the elevator and I was waiting on the stairs and looked to see who it was—well, I'm satisfied it was a woman."

"Still wearing an overcoat?"

"No, the overcoat was over her arm at that time."

"So then *you* went on upstairs?"

"Went on upstairs and waited in front of Brogan's apartment."

"For how long?"

"For a little while. Just like I told you. Then I was satisfied that—well, I thought the figure that went out *must* have been Dad. Please understand me, Mr. Mason, I really and truly thought I was trailing Dad all the time."

"Well," Mason said, "the first thing we have to do is to get Hattie's story."

Sylvia shook her head. "I'm afraid we can't, not until after we've determined our strategy."

"Why not?"

"The police have her."

"The police!" Mason exclaimed. "Why, the doctor said—"

"They wakened her, put her under arrest and bundled her off before the poor girl knew what was happening."

"She'd been drugged," Mason said. "They had no right doing that. Who did it?"

"Sergeant Holcomb."

"Go on," Mason said.

"They—they found the ice pick."

"What ice pick?"

"The one that murdered Fritch."

"Where?"

"In the drawer in Hattie' dresser, underneath her handkerchiefs—the same drawer where I'd concealed the spool of tape, only this was *under* the handkerchiefs. I'd put the tape on *top* of them."

"Well now, *isn't* that interesting," Mason said dryly.

Sylvia said, "I know what you must think of me, Mr. Mason. Probably you think I'm the worst little scatter-brained idiot in the world, but—well, we're into it now, and we're going to have to hang together on this thing."

She opened her purse, took out her checkbook. She said, "I gave you one check for five hundred dollars as a retainer. I'm going to

give you fifteen hundred dollars more, Mr. Mason. I want you to—
to represent Hattie."

Mason watched her filling out the check.

"And please, Mr. Mason," she went on, "please do what I told
you. Remember what I said—I don't want to do anything that
would be a black spot on Dad's memory, but, after all, Fritch *was*
a blackmailer and he *deserved* to die. UnderDad's moral code he
would have been perfectly entitled to kill him.

"If this thing had happened years ago in Texas, Dad wouldn't
have thought anything about pulling a gun and killing J.J. on sight
and no jury would have done anything to him."

"This didn't happen years ago and it isn't in Texas," Mason said.
"And the ideas you had about your father's killing Fritch have all
turned out to be demonstrable fallacies."

"I know, but—well, Dad's gone now. They can't do anything to
punish *him,* and it's better to have a black spot on his memory than
to have one of us girls, I mean, Hattie, in a pack of trouble.

"I'm trying to tell you, Mr. Mason, that since I've already said
what I did about Dad—well, no one knows *all* the details.

"Jarrett has, of course, messed things up. But if someone would
fake a wire to him telling him of a new archaeological discovery in
the jungle, Jarrett would go rushing off without waiting for anything. The funeral wouldn't stop him. He's seen so much of dead
civilizations, he looks on individual death as just a—"

"Now look," Mason interrupted, "you've messed things up
enough. Don't go sending Jarrett any fake wires."

"Why, Mr. Mason! I wouldn't do that. I want you to handle
things now."

Mason said, "Just what *do* you want me to do? What's this check
for?"

"I want you to defend Hattie."

Mason said to Della Street, "Endorse on the back of that
check that it is for the purpose of defending Hattie Bain, and
that I have a free hand to handle the case in my own way, and
if I have an opportunity I am at liberty to expose the murderer,

whoever that murderer may be. Underscore 'whoever that murderer may be.'"

Mason looked up at Sylvia Atwood. "Is that satisfactory?" he asked.

Her green eyes met his steadily. "Why, of course, Mr. Mason," she said. "Why shouldn't it be?"

Mason held her eyes. "We're all in a mess now," he said. "Some of it is due to your desire to be, to quote your brother, little Miss Fix-It. Now try not to send any fake wire or do anything else that will complicate the situation."

"But, Mr. Mason, I think you're terribly conservative. If Jarrett weren't here to testify about seeing Dad they couldn't *prove* it wasn't Dad who went to that apartment. I can swear in all honesty and in all good faith I was trailing Dad."

Mason grinned. "Well, thank you for the compliment."

"What compliment?"

"Thinking I'm too conservative. Tell that to the police some time, will you?"

"You're making fun of me now."

"It's not fun. You're dangerous. I want one thing out of you. Keep your mouth shut and keep your fingers out of the pie."

"I think you're horrid. You've been listening to Jarrett. Before this case is over you'll have reason to thank me for thinking ahead and doing the things your stuffy sense of professional ethics keeps you from even thinking of, much less doing!"

And she walked from the office, head high, shoulders squared.

"Heaven deliver us if she tries anything else!" Mason said.

"Want to bet?" Della asked.

"Good Lord, no!" Mason groaned.

CHAPTER 13

Perry Mason sat in the visitors' room in the jail, looking across at Hattie Bain.

Between them was a heavy partition of plate glass. A microphone and a miniature loud-speaker on each side enabled voices to be heard through the glass screen. Aside from that the parties were as much separated as though they had been in different countries.

Hattie Bain's face showed the devastating effects of the grief at her father's death, the nervous strain to which she had been subjected, and the shock of her imprisonment.

"How are you feeling?" Mason asked.

"Pretty bad. How do I look?"

"Not bad."

"My pictures in the papers were terrible."

"You were full of drugs."

"They didn't give me the breaks at all."

"Did you talk to them?"

"Why, of course, I answered their questions," she said simply.

"Well, suppose you tell me what happened. Did you go to see J.J. Fritch the night of the murder?"

"Yes."

"When?"

"After everything had quieted down at the house. I waited until Dad was asleep and Sylvia had gone to bed."

"Why did you go, Hattie?"

"I thought I could make some deal with him."

"Could you?"

"No."

"Where did you see him, in Brogan's apartment?"

"No, in his apartment. He was nasty to me, insulting to Dad. He was a thoroughly despicable man."

"You told the police all this?"

"Certainly."

"All right, tell me just what happened."

"I drove up to that apartment house. I went up to the apartment that was rented in the name of Frank Reedy, the one that was really Fritch's apartment."

"You knew Fritch?"

"Oh yes, I'd known him years ago when he and Dad were in business together."

"Go on," Mason said.

She said, "I rang the doorbell. I had to ring several times before—"

"That was the Reedy apartment?" Mason asked.

"Yes."

"Now how about the apartment across the hall, the one occupied by George Brogan?"

"J.J. took me in there. He wanted to get me out of his apartment. I think he wasn't alone, that someone was in his apartment. He hustled me right across the hall to that other apartment."

"I want you to think carefully about this," Mason said. "Did you notice any note on the door of that apartment? Anything pinned to the door?"

She thought for a moment, then said, "I can't be certain, Mr. Mason. I was thinking about—yes, I guess perhaps there was."

"But you can't be certain?"

"No, I can't be certain."

"All right, what did you do after you reached Brogan's apartment?"

She said, "I told J.J. that I was going to put the cards right on the table, that you were in a position to prove he was a blackmailer, that you were terribly clever, that he had a tape recording and that you were going to be able to prove it was a forgery.

"I told him that what he was doing was killing Dad without doing himself any good, and I asked him to be a man and not be a sniveling, sneaking blackmailer."

"What happened?"

"He became insulting."

"Then what?"

"He virtually threw me out. He said if we didn't get rid of you we'd all be sorry."

"And then?"

"Then I went home and went to bed."

"Were you wearing your father's coat?"

"Yes, I was. I started out and realized I'd forgotten to bring a wrap, so I opened the closet and grabbed the first thing handy."

"And you told the police all this?"

"Certainly. It's their business to investigate. They have to ask questions. It's the duty of a good citizen to cooperate."

Mason remained thoughtfully silent. Hattie Bain raised dark, steady eyes to his.

"That's the truth," she said.

"And you told it *all* to the police?"

She nodded.

Mason sighed. "Well, we *may* be able to keep the admission out of evidence on the ground that you were filled up with drugs."

"I don't want it kept out of evidence," she said. "I want the truth told just the way it is."

"And what time was this?" Mason asked.

"Between midnight and—I was back about half-past one or two in the morning. I didn't look at my watch."

"What time did you leave Fritch?"

"I can't tell about the exact time."

Mason said, "Now look, I don't want you to make any more statements to anyone. I'm going to try to get you an immediate hearing in court. I'm going to try to at least get the facts straightened out so we know where we stand. Now you aren't lying to protect your father, are you?"

She shook her head.

"Well, we'll do the best we can."

She said, "I haven't any money to pay you, Mr. Mason, unless of course, you could wait for Dad's estate."

Mason said, "Your sister Sylvia retained me to represent you."

For a moment there was some peculiar expression in her eyes. "You're going to do what Sylvia instructs you to do? You're going to let her direct my defense?"

Mason said, "I'm going to handle your defense to the best of my ability. I'm going to be working for you and for you alone. Look at me, Miss Bain. Look me in the eyes. Do you understand what I'm saying?"

"Yes."

"Do you understand that I mean it? That I mean every word of it?"

"Yes."

"All right," Mason said. "Remember it. You're my client and I'm your lawyer. I'm not representing anybody else. Just you."

"Thank you, Mr. Mason."

CHAPTER 14

The courtroom was packed with spectators who appreciated the importance of the legal battle that was about to take place.

Judge Kaylor emerged from his chambers to take his place on the bench. The bailiff rapped the court to order.

"The case of People versus Harriet Bain," Judge Kaylor said.

"Ready for the prosecution," Delbert Moon, a deputy district attorney answered.

"And for the defense," Mason announced.

"This is the preliminary hearing on a charge of first-degree murder," Judge Kaylor said.

Delbert Moon, suave, quick-witted, adroit, one of the newer and more skillful trial deputies in a reorganized district attorney's office, was on his feet.

"If the Court please," he said, "I'll call Mr. George Brogan as my first witness."

George Brogan came forward and was sworn.

He gave his name and address to the clerk, and his occupation as that of a private investigator.

"You were acquainted with an individual known to you as J.J. Fritch in his lifetime?" Moon asked.

"Yes, sir."

"Where is he?"

"He is dead."

"How do you know he is dead?"

"I saw his dead body."

"That's all."

Brogan started to leave the stand.

"Just a moment," Mason said. "I have some cross-examination."

"Now, if the Court please," Moon said, "I have deliberately framed my questions so that this witness, who will be recalled later as a material witness for the prosecution, has at the present time testified only to one phase of the *corpus delicti*. I insist that Counsel confine his cross-examination to that part of the case."

Mason said, "I don't think Counsel needs to advise me how to conduct my cross-examination. I suggest that the orderly procedure is for him to listen to my questions and object to any question that he feels is not proper cross-examination."

"Proceed," Judge Kaylor said, smiling slightly.

"You say that you saw the body of J.J. Fritch?" Mason asked.

"That is right."

"*When* did you see it?"

"I saw it at the morgue."

"Who was present?"

"Sergeant Holcomb of Homicide, and Dr. Hanover, the autopsy surgeon."

"You had known J.J. Fritch in his lifetime?"

"Yes, sir."

"For approximately how long?"

"For a good many years."

"Can you estimate the period of time?"

"No, sir, I cannot."

"Why?"

"It's been a long time."

"Five years?"

"Yes."

"Ten years?"

"Perhaps."

"Fifteen years?"

"I don't know."

"More than ten years?"

"I couldn't say."

"Can't you tell when you first met Mr. Fritch?"

"No, sir, I cannot remember."

"Now you state that you saw the body of Mr. Fritch in the morgue?"

"Yes, sir."

"Was that the *first* time you had seen the dead body of Mr. Fritch?"

"Now, Your Honor," Moon said, "I object. The witness has been called solely for the purpose of establishing the fact that J.J. Fritch was known by him in his lifetime, and that J.J. Fritch is dead. Our next witness will be Dr. Hanover, the autopsy surgeon, who will prove Mr. Fritch met his death by violence at the hands of some third person. We will then be in a position to proceed in an orderly way to connect up the defendant with the death of J.J. Fritch. Therefore, this question is not proper cross-examination at this time. Later on, when the witness has appeared and given his testimony in detail concerning other phases of the case, the question may well be proper."

"The question is quite proper at this time," Mason said. "You asked the witness if he saw the body of J.J. Fritch. I am asking him when he saw the body, and I am asking him when *he first* saw the body."

"The objection is overruled," Judge Kaylor said.

"When did you first see the body?" Mason asked.

Brogan shifted his position slightly, took a deep breath, glanced over Mason's head at the back of the courtroom, then down at the floor.

"Can't you answer that question?" Mason asked.

"I was trying to get the thing fixed in my mind, trying to get it clear in my mind."

"Well, take your time," Mason said. "Take just as long as you want."

Brogan hesitated for a moment, looked at the deputy district attorney, then glanced away, then said, "As nearly as I can remember it, it was approximately five minutes past nine on the morning of the seventh of this month."

"Where was that body?"

"It was lying on the floor of my apartment in front of the door leading to a closet where I stored liquor."

"What was the condition of the body?"

"Now then, if the Court please," Moon said, "I am again going to object. This is all matter which can be brought out when Mr. Brogan is called as a witness on the other phase of our case. It is not proper at the present time."

Mason said, "The witness has been asked on direct examination as to whether he knew J.J. Fritch and whether he saw the body. I am asking him now to describe the body. I certainly have that right."

"I think so," Judge Kaylor said. "The objection is overruled. Answer the question."

"Go ahead," Mason said, "answer the question."

"The upper part of the body was stiff. It was slightly doubled, that is, the elbows were doubled and pressed into the sides. The body was clad in underwear and that's all."

"Anything else you can think of about the body?"

"There were several small puncture wounds."

"You noticed them at that time?"

"No, sir, I did not, but I noticed little stains of dry blood on the undershirt."

"What kind of an undershirt?"

"A ribbed, sleeveless, athletic undershirt."

"What can you say about the color of the body?"

"Why, nothing. It was sort of a grayish color, the color of a corpse."

"What about the back? Did you notice any color on the back?"

"There was—now that you mention it, I think there was a bruise on the back—below the neck—between the shoulders."

"Visible under the undershirt?"

"Yes, sir. The head was twisted a little. The body was on its back."

"Now that's relating to the time you first saw the body?"

"Yes, sir."

"Now let's go to the next time you saw the body, where was that?"

"That was when it was in the morgue."

"What was the condition of the body at that time?"

"It had been stretched out."

"You could recognize the features?"

"Yes, sir."

"Was that before the autopsy or afterward?"

"Immediately before the autopsy."

"Now, Mr. Brogan," Mason said, "when I asked you when you had first seen the body you hesitated perceptibly. Do you remember that?"

"Oh, if the Court please," Moon said, "I think that is not proper cross-examination, and furthermore I don't think the witness hesitated."

Mason said, "The witness did hesitate, and furthermore he stated when I asked him why he was hesitating that he was trying to get the thing fixed in his mind, trying to get it clear in his mind."

"I believe that is correct," Judge Kaylor ruled.

"Why did you hesitate?" Mason asked.

"I was trying to collect my thoughts on the subject."

"Were your thoughts scattered?"

"The expression was figurative."

"Why did you have to stop and study in order to remember what time it was when you *first* saw the body?"

"I wanted to be certain I wasn't mistaken."

"Thank you," Mason said. "Now I want to ask you a few questions about your acquaintanceship with J.J. Fritch. You can't remember the time you first met him?"

"No, sir."

"Had you done any business for Mr. Fritch?"

"I was—no, not *for* Mr. Fritch, no."

"He had consulted you in connection with a business matter shortly before his death?"

"I will express it this way, Mr. Mason. I know what you're trying to get at and I'll say—"

"Now never mind trying to anticipate what I'm getting at," Mason said. "I have asked you a simple question. I want you to answer it."

"Well, I was not representing J.J. Fritch."

"Whom were you representing?"

"I actually was not representing anyone."

"You were trying to get Sylvia Atwood, the sister of the defendant, to retain you?"

"Yes, sir."

"For what purpose?"

"To secure possession of a tape recording which I felt might be quite damaging to the family."

"Who originally approached you in that connection?"

"I approached Mrs. Atwood."

"Who originally approached you?"

"Mr. Fritch."

"What did he want?"

"He thought that it might be possible to get some money out of the Bain family in return for a tape recording."

"You had heard that tape recording?"

"Yes, sir."

"Did you know there was more than one tape recording?"

"Well—there had been—I believe there was only one original."

"But you did know that one or more copies had been made?"

Moon was on his feet. "*Now,* Your Honor, I am quite certain this cross-examination has gone far afield. Counsel is trying to present his own case by cross-examining my witness. Counsel will hear plenty about that tape recording in a short time when Counsel is called to the stand to explain how that tape recording came to be in *his* possession."

Judge Kaylor said, "The Court is going to ask Counsel to refrain from these acrimonious, sarcastic personalities. The objection is sustained."

Mason smiled at the worried Brogan.

"Thank you, Mr. Brogan," Mason said. "That's all."

"No further questions," Moon said. "Call Dr. Hanover."

Dr. Hanover came forward, was sworn, gave his name, residence and occupation, and a brief summary of his professional qualifications.

"I ask you, Dr. Hanover," Moon said, "if you were present when a body was identified by Mr. George Brogan, the witness who has just left the stand?"

"I was. Yes, sir."

"That was the body that he has now identified as being that of J.J. Fritch?"

"Yes, sir."

"Doctor, when did you first see the body in question?"

"At approximately nine-forty on the morning of the seventh."

"Did you at that time make preliminary tests to determine when death had occurred?"

"I did. Yes, sir."

"And what did those tests show?"

"That death had occurred between midnight and three o'clock in the morning of that same day."

"Did you subsequently perform a post-mortem on that body?"

"I did. Yes, sir."

"Doctor, I don't want a technical description of what you found—I want you to just tell the Court in plain, ordinary language as to what you found was the cause of death."

"The cause of death was a series of eight puncture wounds which had penetrated the chest cavity. Four of those wounds had been made from the front and two of them had penetrated the heart. Four of the wounds had been made from behind. One of them had penetrated the heart, two the lung, one had failed to penetrate because of striking the clavicle, or shoulder blade."

"Those wounds caused the death?"

"Yes, sir."

"An immediate death?"

"That depends on what you mean by the word immediate. I would say that the *immediate* effect of the wounds was to cause the man to fall forward, to become helpless. Death ensued within a relatively short time."

"Now then," Moon said, "I'm going to ask you if you are acquainted with a phenomenon known technically as post-mortem lividity?"

"I am. Yes, sir."

"Will you please explain what is meant by that?"

"Yes, sir. After death, when the blood ceases to circulate in the body, it naturally has a tendency while it is still fluid to settle to the lowest portion of the body. This causes a congestion of the blood vessels in the underside of the body, and as the blood undergoes the changes which are associated with a cessation of circulation, I might say a stagnation if I were to use a term that might make it more understandable, there is a discoloration or a lividity in the portion of the body affected. To the uninitiated that may seem to be a bruise."

"Now, Doctor, where does this post-mortem lividity form?"

"Upon the parts of the body that are affected by the settling of blood due to gravitational attraction."

"You mean by that the lowest portions of the body?"

"That is correct. Speaking from a standpoint of body position and not from a standpoint of anatomical structure. In other words, if the body is left lying on its back the postmortem lividity will appear along the muscles of the back, particularly the places where the skin is pressing against some object."

"If the body is lying on its stomach the post-mortem lividity will not be on the back?"

"No, sir."

"And if the body is propped in such a position so that it is sitting straight up, would you expect to find a post-mortem lividity between the shoulders or along the back of the neck?"

"No, sir."

"Did you find any post-mortem lividity on the body of J.J. Fritch?"

"I did, sir. A very well defined post-mortem lividity."

"And where was this located? I'm going to ask you, Doctor, just to indicate and explain in ordinary language if you will, please, disregarding anatomical terms as much as possible."

Dr. Hanover placed his right hand to the back of his neck between the shoulder blades, said, "There was some postmortem lividity here and in two or three places along the back."

"What did this post-mortem lividity indicate to you as an autopsy surgeon and an experienced pathologist, Doctor?"

"That the body had been lying on its back."

"Now what about *rigor mortis?*"

"*Rigor mortis* had set in to the extent that the arms and shoulders were locked in *rigor mortis,* but *rigor mortis* had not as yet proceeded to the legs."

"That is, when the body was found?"

"Yes, sir."

"Returning to post-mortem lividity, Doctor, when does it begin to form?"

"Under most conditions this discoloration will begin to be apparent from one to two hours after death."

"And what can you tell us about the development of *rigor mortis,* Doctor?"

"*Rigor mortis* develops first in the face and jaws. The onset usually takes place in this area in from three to five hours after death. The rigidity gradually extends downward, involving the neck, chest and arms, abdomen, and finally the legs and feet. For the entire body to be involved usually requires a period of from about eight to twelve hours after death.

"However, *rigor mortis* is a variable factor. It depends somewhat upon circumstances, perhaps somewhat upon temperature."

"From your observations, taken as a whole, Doctor, can you fix the time of death of the body in question?"

"Yes, sir. I can fix it within a period of three hours."

"And those three hours are what?"

"Between midnight and 3:00 A.M."

"Cross-examine," Moon said.

"Did you," Mason asked, "fix the time of death solely from the development of *rigor mortis*"?

"No, sir. I did not."

"Did you fix it from the post-mortem lividity?"

"Definitely not."

"Let us suppose that a body had been lying in one position long enough for post-mortem lividity to have formed. Then someone moved the body. Would that change the postmortem lividity?"

"Definitely that would not. When the blood has once settled there is a certain amount of clotting which takes place in the tissues, so that if the body is moved after this has taken place the original lividity will still be present.

"As one of the outstanding authorities has stated in a book on the subject, when a dead body is found with post-mortem lividity on the upper surface of the body the investigator can be sure that someone has moved that body from its position at a time at least several hours after death occurred. There again, Mr. Mason, when I refer to the upper portion of the body I mean the upper positional portion rather than the upper anatomical portion."

"I understand," Mason said. "As I understand it, Doctor, you are not basing your conclusions as to the time of death entirely on the post-mortem lividity?"

"No, sir. That is a factor, but post-mortem lividity and *rigor mortis* are somewhat indefinite factors. *Rigor mortis* varies considerably in connection with the time of development. If a person dies after a fight, or after extreme muscular exertion, *rigor mortis* may set in very quickly. For myself I consider it rather dangerous to try to predicate a conclusion as to time of death entirely upon *rigor mortis*.

"That, of course, refers to fixing a time of death within the narrow limits of one hour, two hours or three hours. Of course, over a longer period of time a person can make an estimate, and a very accurate estimate, for instance, a six-hour period during which death must have occurred. After twenty-four hours, if certain characteristic changes in *rigor mortis* are present, I would say that it would be possible to draw a conclusion as to a six-hour interval during which death must have taken place."

"But in this case you are fixing it within a three-hour period?"

"Yes, sir."

"Doctor, you probably know your own mind better than anyone. I'm going to ask you if you are prejudiced against the defendant in this case?"

Dr. Hanover gave the question frowning consideration. "Well, of course, I have an opinion as to the guilt or innocence of the defendant."

"You think she is guilty?"

"I do."

"That is a fixed opinion in your mind?"

"It is."

"Due to investigations you have made?"

"Investigations I have made and investigations that have been made by others and the results of which I know."

"Therefore you are prejudiced against the defendant?"

"I don't think I am prejudiced against her. I have an opinion as to her guilt."

"And as a citizen you would dislike to see a guilty defendant escape the penalty of her crime?"

"That is right."

"Therefore, since you feel the defendant is guilty, you are anxious to see that she pays the penalty?"

"I suppose that is true."

"So that in giving your testimony you would naturally try to give it in such a way as to bring about the greatest prejudice to the defendant's case?"

"No, sir, that very definitely is not correct."

"I am not talking now, Doctor, about altering the *facts*. I am talking about the *manner* of giving your testimony."

"Yes, sir."

"Now, Doctor, may I ask you what factors you have taken into consideration in connection with fixing the time of death during this three-hour period?"

"Two factors," Dr. Hanover said. "The time element involved in connection with the ingestion of a meal, which I naturally assume was a normal evening meal, and the temperature of the body. The temperature factor I consider an absolute index."

"You didn't mention either of these matters on direct examination, Doctor."

"I wasn't asked about them."

"You were asked as to fixing the time of death?"

"I was, and I fixed the time of death."

"Now, Doctor, did you know that you were not going to be asked about these two other factors on your direct examination?"

"Oh, Your Honor," Moon said, "I think this is not legitimate cross-examination. This is nagging at the witness, bickering with the witness. This is splitting hairs with the witness. This is dragging in completely irrelevant matters."

"No, it isn't," Mason said. "This is going to the question of the bias of the witness."

"He has already testified that he thinks the defendant is guilty, and he wants to see her convicted," Moon said.

"Exactly," Mason retorted, "but he has also sworn under his oath that the prejudice didn't in any way affect the manner in which he gave his testimony. I now propose to show that it has affected the manner in which he's giving his testimony."

"Just how do you mean, Mr. Mason?" Judge Kaylor asked.

"I propose to show," Mason said, "that Dr. Hanover deliberately refrained from making any statement as to the factors by which he fixed the time of death on direct examination because he had an understanding with the prosecutor that he would carefully refrain from mentioning those two factors on direct examination, thereby trapping me into cross-examining him on the element of time. He felt he would be in a better strategic position to harm the defendant's case by doing this on cross-examination rather than on direct examination."

"The objection is overruled," Judge Kaylor said.

"Can you answer that question, Doctor?" Mason asked.

Dr. Hanover suddenly became uncomfortable.

"Well," he said, "I had, of course, discussed my testimony with the authorities."

"By the authorities you mean the deputy district attorney?"

"And the police."

"But with the deputy district attorney?"

"Yes, sir."

"And did the police tell you anything about the manner in which you were to give your testimony?"

Dr. Hanover rose at once to the bait. "Absolutely not, sir. They did not. There is absolutely nothing to justify that insinuation."

"Did the deputy district attorney?" Mason asked.

Abruptly Dr. Hanover became embarrassed. "Well, there was a general discussion as to what my testimony would cover."

"Wasn't there a *specific* discussion that you would say nothing on direct examination as to the manner in which you fixed the time of death, that you would simply give a flat opinion that death occurred between midnight and three o'clock in the morning, that you would purposely refrain from elaborating on your reasons, and that when I cross-examined you you would then be in a position to crucify me?"

"I don't think the word crucify was used."

"But its equivalent?"

"Well, I will say that I was instructed to—no, instructed is not the right word. I am somewhat at a loss for the right word. It was agreed that I would withhold testimony as to details until the questions were asked on cross-examination."

"Forcing me to lead with my chin?" Mason asked.

Dr. Hanover smiled. "That is a slang expression which was not used."

"All right, what was the slang expression that *was* used?" Mason asked.

Dr. Hanover abruptly shifted his eyes and remained silent.

"Oh, Your Honor," Moon said, "I think the exact words are immaterial. Dr. Hanover has certainly given Counsel the point Counsel was trying so laboriously to make."

"I want the exact words," Mason said. "I think I'm entitled to have them. I think it has a bearing on the attitude of this witness."

"The objection is overruled."

"What was the exact slang expression that was used?'"

"Nail you to the cross," Dr. Hanover blurted.

"So that when you smiled in rather a superior manner and said that the word crucify was not used, you were taking advantage of a technicality?"

"I object to that question as argumentative," Moon said.

"Sustained," Judge Kaylor ruled. "The facts speak for themselves."

"Now then," Mason said, abruptly shifting his tactics, "you stated that the immediate effect of the wounds was not to cause death but would cause the man to fall forward and become helpless?"

"I believe I so testified. Yes, sir."

"That is your opinion?"

"Yes, sir."

"Fall *forward!*" Mason asked.

"Yes, sir."

"Why do you assume he fell forward rather than backward?"

"Because I am assuming that the four stab wounds in front were the first wounds and that after the man fell forward the other four wounds were inflicted while he was lying on his face."

"And why do you assume that?"

"Why, because it's—it's natural."

"And why do you say it's natural?"

"Well, frankly, there is nothing about any of the wounds that would enable me to tell the order in which the wounds had been inflicted. They were all inflicted at approximately the same time, that is, in what I would judge a rapid sequence, but if the man was stabbed in the heart and fell forward it would be impossible to inflict any more stabs in the front, and the remaining four stabs would have been in the back."

"Unless," Mason said, "the first four stabs had been in the back and the man had fallen over backward, in which event the remaining four wounds would have been in the front."

"Well, have it that way if you want to."

"I don't want to have it either way," Mason said. "All I want to bring out is the fact that beyond mere surmise and conjecture you know nothing as to the order in which the wounds were inflicted or whether the wounds in front were first or those in back were second."

"I was assuming that the wounds in front were made first, but I will admit, Mr. Mason, that I cannot testify to that."

"And yet you have just testified that the post-mortem lividity indicated the body had been *lying on its back*?"

"Well—yes, when the body finally came to rest."

"And death presupposes that?"

"Oh, I suppose so."

"So then the evidence you have uncovered from your examination indicates the first four wounds were the back wounds."

"It could be."

"I am asking you if the evidence you uncovered in your examination doesn't so indicate."

"Yes, I guess it does."

"Don't guess, Doctor. Does it?"

"Yes, but that evidence isn't sufficient to be conclusive."

"Then you don't know in what position the man died?"

"No, sir."

"But you assume the body had been moved after death?"

"Definitely not. I don't think it had been."

"Then the attack must have been from the rear."

"I won't argue the point, Mr. Mason."

"Don't argue, answer."

"Well—I don't know."

"Then you don't know the man fell forward?"

"No."

"Did you examine the body for poisons?"

"I examined the body for the cause of death. I found the cause of death to be the series of puncture wounds mentioned before."

"You found they were sufficient to cause death?"

"Yes, sir."

"Do you know, of your own knowledge, whether there was any other contributing cause of death, such as poison?"

"No, sir. I know that these wounds were inflicted during the man's lifetime. I know that the result of those wounds would have been to produce death. Therefore, I assume that those wounds were the cause of death. Whether there was any other factor which would cause symptoms I do not know. I do know that the wounds were the cause of death. That is what I was asked about and that's what I testified about."

"Now, Doctor, you state that you have determined the time of death as being between midnight and three o'clock on the morning of the seventh."

"Yes, sir."

"That is an accurate determination?"

"Understand, Mr. Mason, I cannot tell *exactly* when death occurred, but I *can* fix limits *within which death must have occurred*. I am prepared to state that death did not occur prior to midnight and that it did not occur after three o'clock on the morning of the seventh. I think the probabilities are that death occurred around one o'clock in the morning, but in order to be on the safe side I have established that three-hour limit and am prepared to state that death occurred somewhere within those three hours."

"How do you know?" Mason asked.

"Primarily by taking the temperature of the body and comparing it with certain statistical information we have as to the rate of cooling."

"And," Mason said, smiling, "this is the phase of your testimony that you and the prosecutor's office decided could best be brought out on cross-examination?"

"Well, yes."

"All right then, let's bring it out. What about the rate of cooling?"

"The average normal temperature of a body at the time of death, particularly in case of a death by violence, may be assumed as ninety-eight point six Fahrenheit. The body will cool at the rate of approximately one and one-half degrees an hour, depending upon surrounding circumstances—for the first twelve hours, that is."

"Why do you say in cases of homicide?"

"Because in cases of natural death the man may have been suffering from a high fever. If, for instance, there was a fever of a hundred and three this would make a difference in the body temperature and so would affect calculations as to the time of death. On the other hand, where a man is apparently in perfect health at the time of death and meets a violent end, we are safe in assuming a temperature of ninety-eight point six."

"So you determined the time of death in this case because of the temperature of the body?"

"Primarily. I also took into consideration the extent to which *rigor mortis* had developed, the state of food in the digestive tract, and the appearance of the post-mortem lividity."

"Did you take into consideration the fact that the body was unclothed?"

"Yes, sir. I took into consideration the various elements of temperature. In other words, the temperature of the surrounding air, and the fact that the body was unclothed."

"But *was* the body unclothed at the time of death?" Mason asked.

"I am assuming that it was."

"That is an assumption like the one you made about the sequence of the wounds, Doctor, simply predicated upon what seems to your mind to be most natural?"

"No, sir. We made a most careful examination of the clothing that was hanging in the closet of the apartment occupied by the decedent."

"That apartment was directly across the hall from the apartment occupied by George Brogan?"

"That is correct."

"You examined that clothing very carefully?"

"All of it, yes, sir."

"Looking for what?"

"For puncture marks or bloodstains."

"You found neither?"

"No, sir."

"Therefore at the time of death you are prepared to state that J.J. Fritch was wandering around the apartment of George Brogan clad only in an undershirt and shorts?"

"No, sir, I am not."

"I thought that was the effect of your testimony."

"I can't state that he was wandering around. I will further state this, Mr. Mason, *if the* body *had* been clothed, and if the clothing had been removed at some time shortly after death, the determination as to the time of death because of temperature rate would not have been changed. I am making a sufficient allowance in the three-hour time limit so that I feel certain death did not occur before midnight and did not occur after 3:00 A.M."

"Those are absolute time limits?" Mason asked.

"Absolutely. Yes, sir."

"You are satisfied that it was a physical impossibility for death to have occurred before midnight?"

"Yes."

"Or later than three o'clock in the morning?"

"Yes, sir."

"You are prepared to stake your reputation on that, Doctor?"

"I am testifying to it."

"Thank you," Mason said. "That is all."

Moon said, "Just a moment, Doctor. I have a few questions to ask you on redirect examination covering points that were brought out by Mr. Mason in his cross-examination. Now, Doctor, when you first saw this body, where was it?"

"It was lying on the floor in the apartment of George Brogan."

"Where in that apartment?"

"Immediately in front of a liquor closet, and I may state the person who claimed to have found the body claimed that it had been in the liquor closet and had tumbled out when the door was opened."

"Just a moment," Mason said, "I move to strike the last part of that out as being hearsay."

"Objection sustained. The motion is granted. That part of the testimony will be stricken," Judge Kaylor ruled.

Moon, nettled but realizing that his position was legally indefensible, accepted his defeat as gracefully as possible, and said, "Would it have been possible, Doctor, in your opinion, for this body to have been placed in that liquor closet and to have fallen out when the door was opened?"

"No, sir."

"Why?"

"Taking into consideration the various factors which I have enumerated, that assumption is completely negatived."

"Why?"

"Because, in the first place, it is negatived by the position of the arms. *Rigor mortis* had developed so that the arms were locked in position. The elbows were close to the sides. The hands were near the jaw. Yet there was no evidence that the arms had been tied up in any way."

"And what does that indicate, Doctor?"

"That the body very definitely could not have been propped up in the liquor closet, or anywhere else, immediately after death. The hands and arms in that case would have dropped, and *rigor mortis* would have set in, locking the arms in that lower position. The fact that the hands were elevated, that the elbows were at the sides, indicates that the body must have been lying on its back rather than propped up. In my opinion, that was the only way in which *rigor mortis* could have set in with the hands in that position."

"Any other reasons?"

"Yes, sir, the development of post-mortem lividity."

"Thank you, Doctor, that's all."

"Now, just a minute," Mason said. "I'd like to ask the doctor a few more questions about that."

"Very well, go right ahead," Moon said.

"This was testimony that you had previously discussed with the prosecutor?"

"Yes, sir."

"And had agreed between you that if necessary it was to be brought out on redirect examination, but that you would try while you were being cross-examined to slip in the fact that the person who found the body claimed it had tumbled out of the liquor closet?"

"Well, that's a fact. I heard that statement myself."

"At the time the body was discovered?"

"At a later date. I interviewed that witness."

"But it was agreed that you were to try to slip that fact in on cross-examination?"

"Well—I—I pointed out that that statement of the witness was obviously false, and Mr. Moon suggested that if possible I should point that out while I was giving my testimony."

"And was it suggested that you slip that statement in if you had a chance?"

"Oh, Your Honor, I think we've gone into this a dozen times," Moon said. "Let's assume that this witness is favorable to the prosecution."

"On that assumption," Mason said, "I won't insist on an answer. I simply want the Court to understand that the entire testimony of this witness is colored by a prejudice in favor of the prosecution."

"That isn't what I said," Moon said.

"But that's what *I* say," Mason said, "and if there's any question about it I'll continue to bore into this witness until it is established."

"Oh, go ahead. Let's get the case over with," Moon said, sitting down. "It's a minor point. I don't care one way or the other."

"It wouldn't have been possible," Mason asked, "for the body to have been placed in the liquor closet, the hands raised and then the door closed holding the hands in position?"

"You couldn't have held the hands in that position while you were closing the door without the use of some kind of a device that would tie the hands up," Dr. Hanover said, "and even then you wouldn't have a condition of post-mortem lividity such as I found. Taking the two together there is absolutely no question but what the body lay on its back after death in approximately the position in which it was found by the police."

"Did you examine the carpet to see if there were any traces of blood?"

"You mean in front of the liquor closet?"

"Where the body was lying."

"Yes, sir. I did."

"Did you find such traces?"

"No."

"That's all, Doctor."

"Just a moment," Moon said. "Would you have expected to find such traces, Doctor?"

"Not necessarily. The bleeding was very minute due to the small nature of the puncture wounds, which sealed themselves almost immediately. There was some internal hemorrhage but very little external hemorrhage. It is quite possible that the undershirt would have absorbed all of the visible traces of blood."

"Thank you, that's all."

"Just one more question," Mason said, smiling. "You have some very delicate tests for ascertaining presence of blood, do you not, Doctor?"

"Yes, sir."

"Tests that will show microscopic quantities of blood, very microscopic quantities?"

"Well, they're not specific, but they *do* show blood. They show several things and blood is one of them."

"Were those tests performed on this carpet?"

"No, sir. We looked the carpet over but found no signs of blood."

"Why weren't those tests made on the carpet?"

"Very frankly we didn't think of it at the time, Mr. Mason. It was assumed when the police first saw the body that the statement made by the witness was correct and that the body had tumbled out of the liquor closet when the door was opened. It wasn't until later on that the post-mortem examination indicated definitely that statement could not have been true. By that time there had been quite a bit of trampling around over the carpet, the conditions were not the same as when the body was discovered, and the prosecutor's office felt that that would make any evidence we might try to produce objectionable—the fact that the carpet hadn't been preserved in the same condition and that people had walked over it."

"That's all," Mason said.

"That's all, Doctor," Moon said.

Dr. Hanover withdrew from the stand, obviously relieved that the ordeal was over.

Delbert Moon said, "Call Mrs. Erma Lorton as the prosecution's next witness."

Mrs. Lorton, a tall, angular woman with somewhat close-set eyes and a mouth that was a thin line of determination, came striding forward to the witness stand.

She gave her name and stated that her address was the Mendon Apartments.

"That is the apartment house in which Mr. Brogan and the decedent, Mr. Fritch, had apartments?"

"Yes, sir."

"I'm going to direct your attention to the early hours of the morning of the seventh, Mrs. Lorton," Moon said, arising to his feet, smoothing down his coat, adjusting his hair, looking around at the audience, quite aware of the fact that he was about to explode a dramatic bombshell.

"Yes, sir."

"At about twelve-thirty on the morning of the seventh, what were you doing?"

"I was occupying my apartment."

"And specifically what were you doing?"

"I was waiting up."

"For what purpose?"

"I was waiting for my neighbor to come in."

"By your neighbor, whom do you mean?"

"The one who occupied the adjoining apartment."

"What is your apartment?"

"607."

"And your neighbor occupied what apartment?"

"609."

"Who was this neighbor?"

"A young woman."

"A friend of yours?"

"Yes."

"Now I am not going to ask you anything except a general question to establish the nature of your interest. Had this young woman confided in you as to certain matters? You can answer that question yes or no."

"Yes, she had."

"And was the nature of that confidence such that you would naturally be expected to take an interest in the time she returned home on the night in question?"

"Yes."

"And you were waiting up in order to see what time she returned home?"

"Yes."

"And what, if anything, did you observe?"

"At twelve-thirty-five in the morning I had my door very slightly ajar. I was listening for the sound of the elevator."

"You heard the sound of the elevator?"

"I did. Yes, sir."

"And what happened?"

"When I heard the elevator door clang and steps in the corridor, I assumed it was my friend. I wanted to let her know that I was still up in case I could be of any assistance to her. I opened the door a crack so as to beckon to her."

"And what happened?"

"I found that the steps were not approaching my apartment but that a person was standing in front of the elevator, looking at the numbers on the apartments."

"Can you identify this person?"

"Yes, sir. She was the defendant in this action."

"The one now seated next to Mr. Perry Mason?"

"Yes, sir."

"If the Court please, I'm going to ask the defendant, Harriet Bain, to stand up."

"Stand up," the judge said.

Harriet Bain stood up.

"That is the woman?" Moon asked.

"That is the woman. Yes, sir."

"And did you see what happened to this woman, where she went?"

"Yes, sir. I continued to watch."

"Tell the Court what happened. Where did she go?"

"Down to the end of the hall, to the apartment occupied by Frank Reedy."

"That is, the man whom you then knew as Frank Reedy?"

"Yes, sir."

"And do you now know his real name?"

"Yes, sir."

"What is it?"

"J.J. Fritch."

"I am going to show you a photograph of J.J. Fritch, deceased, and I will ask you if that is the man you knew in his lifetime as Frank Reedy?"

"It is."

"That is his photograph?"

"It is."

"I ask to have this marked for identification, Your Honor."

"So ordered."

"Now, Mrs. Lorton, I am going to ask you what did the defendant do?"

"She rang the bell."

"Of that apartment?"

"Yes."

"And then what happened?"

"She rang the bell two or three times."

"And then what happened?"

"Mr. Reedy, that is, Mr. Fritch opened the door and let her in."

"Did you see her leave that apartment?"

"No, sir."

"You didn't see her come out?"

"No, sir."

"Did you continue to watch for some period of time?"

"Yes, sir."

"For how long?"

"For ten minutes."

"And then what happened?"

"The elevator door opened, my friend came in, and I talked briefly with her. I told her that I was still up and that if she wanted to talk things over with me it would be all right. She told me everything had been adjusted satisfactorily, and so I went to bed."

"You may cross-examine," Moon said.

Mason smiled at the witness.

"You identified the defendant without any trouble?"

"Yes, sir."

"You have exceptionally good eyesight?"

"My eyes are very good. Yes, sir."

"Do you wear glasses?"

"No, sir."

"Do you ever wear glasses?"

"Sometimes for reading, yes."

"Do you wear them always for reading?"

"Well, yes."

"You can see without your glasses?"

"Yes, sir."

"But you can't *read* without them?"

"No, sir."

"You have to wear glasses for reading?"

"It's necessary, yes, sir. I told you that," she snapped angrily.

"And you're not wearing glasses now?"

"No, sir."

"And you were quite able to identify the defendant when she stood up?"

"Yes, sir."

"Was that the first time you had seen the defendant after the seventh of the month?"

"No, sir."

"You had seen her at the jail?"

"Yes, sir."

"In a line-up?"

"No, sir."

"She was by herself?"

"Yes, sir."

"She was pointed out to you?"

"Yes, sir."

"By whom?"

"By Sergeant Holcomb."

"And what did Sergeant Holcomb say to you at that time?"

"Oh, if the Court please, I object to this as not proper cross-examination, as being hearsay evidence," Moon said.

"Sustained," Judge Kaylor said.

"Did someone point out the defendant to you at that time?"

"*I* pointed out the defendant."

"You said that that person was the defendant?"

"Yes, sir."

"But who first directed your attention to the defendant?"

"Well, of course, the police wanted to know if I could identify her. They took me to the jail to see if I could."

There was a slight titter in the courtroom.

"Then the police *first* pointed the defendant out to you and *then* you pointed the defendant out to the police?"

"Well, I agreed she was the person I had seen."

"That was the only person they showed you?"

"Yes, sir."

"Then you were advised at that time, were you not, that that person was Harriet Bain, who had been arrested for the murder of J.J. Fritch?"

"Yes, sir."

"Now then," Mason said, "since you have to wear glasses to read how did it happen that you were able to identify the photograph of J.J. Fritch while you were not wearing your glasses?"

"I—I could see it."

"Could you see it well enough to identify it?"

"Yes, sir."

Mason picked up a law book from the desk, took it up and handed it to her, said, "Just go ahead and read one paragraph, any paragraph, from this page. Read it without your glasses."

She squinted her eyes, held the book far out in front of her, then brought it closer, then back out in front of her again.

"I can't read it," she said. "I can't see it well enough to read it clearly."

"And you couldn't see the photograph any more clearly?"

"I knew whose photograph it was," she replied triumphantly.

"How did you know?"

"The deputy district attorney, Mr. Moon, told me that the photograph he handed me was that of Mr. J.J. Fritch," she said righteously.

"Thank you," Mason said, smiling. "That is all."

Moon, plainly angry, shouted at the witness, "Well, despite the fact you didn't have your glasses on you could see the photograph well enough to know it was the photograph of the man you knew as Frank Reedy, couldn't you?"

"That's objected to," Mason said, "as leading and suggestive."

"This is redirect examination, Your Honor," Moon said.

"It doesn't make any difference what it is," Mason said. "You can't put words in the mouth of your own witness."

"I think you'd better reframe the question," Judge Kaylor said.

"But, of course, Your Honor, in redirect examination it becomes necessary to direct the attention of the witness to the particular part of the testimony brought out on cross-examination that you wish to refute."

"Just ask her the question," Mason said, "but don't put the words in her mouth."

Moon said, "I'm not taking my ruling from you."

"Apparently you're not taking it from the Court either," Mason told him. "The Court has already ruled."

Judge Kaylor said, "Come, come, gentlemen, let's have no personalities. The Court ruled that the objection was well taken. Reframe your question, Mr. Deputy District Attorney."

"You saw that photograph?" Moon asked the witness.

"Yes, sir."

"And recognized it?"

"Yes, sir."

"That's all."

"Just a moment," Mason said. "*How* did you recognize it?"

"Well, I could see that it was a photograph."

"Could you distinguish the features any plainer than you could read the printing in that book I just handed you?"

"Well, I knew it was the photograph because Mr. Moon had told me it was the photograph I'd be called on to identify."

"And you were willing to take his word for it?" Mason said.

"Certainly."

"And similarly," Mason said, "when the officers pointed out the defendant in this case to you and told you that she was the person whom you had seen there in the hallway you were willing to take their word for it, weren't you?"

"Well, it isn't the same situation. I'm *certain* about her."

"Then you weren't certain about the man in the photograph?"

"I could have been dubious. I was taking Mr. Moon's word for it. He'd shown me the same photograph twice before and I'd identified it."

Mason smiled. "How do you know it was the same photograph?"

She snapped angrily, "I guess the word of a district attorney is good enough for me!"

"And, by the same token, so is the word of a sergeant of police?"

"Yes."

"That's all."

"Oh, that's all," Moon said irritably. "We'll get this matter disposed of right now. Call Frank Haswell."

Frank Haswell, a tall, thin individual, with a lazy, good-natured manner, settled himself on the witness stand as though he intended to remain for some time and wanted to be comfortable.

Preliminary questions showed that he was a fingerprint expert, that he had been called on to dust the apartment occupied by George Brogan for latent fingerprints, and that he had made an extensive search of the apartment looking for fingerprints. He had found and photographed a large number.

Moon once more stood up in order to attract the attention of the audience, unmistakably posing, unmistakably rather proud of his own personal appearance, tall, broad-shouldered, slim-waisted, with a wealth of wavy hair sweeping back from his forehead.

"Then, Mr. Haswell," he said, "were you able to identify any of these latent fingerprints that you took?"

"Yes, sir. I was."

"Did you find the fingerprints of any person who is now in this courtroom?"

"Yes, sir."

"Whose?"

Haswell said, "I found the fingerprints of Perry Mason."

Laughter rocked the courtroom despite the attempt of the bailiff to secure order. Even Judge Kaylor permitted himself a smile.

"Where did you find those fingerprints?"

"In three places."

"Where?"

"On the underside of a table in the living room, on the blade of a knife in the kitchen, and on the back of a magnetic knife-holder over the kitchen sink."

"How did you identify those fingerprints?"

"Mr. Mason had previously given a set of prints to the department in connection with another homicide case."

"What other fingerprints did you find?"

"I found the prints of Harriet Bain."

"The defendant in this case?"

"Yes, sir."

"How did you check those fingerprints?"

"By making a direct comparison with original fingerprints from her fingers."

"Where did you find her fingerprints?"

"I could best illustrate that by identifying a photograph of the living room and a photograph of the room where the body was discovered. There are certain places marked on that photograph. Little white circles. Those represent the approximate location of the places where I found the fingerprints of the defendant."

"We would like to offer that photograph in evidence. I will show it to Counsel and—"

"There's no need," Mason said. "I'm only too glad to stipulate that this photograph may be received in evidence."

"Cross-examine," Moon snapped.

"You only found three of my fingerprints?" Mason asked incredulously.

"Yes, sir."

"Why didn't you find more? I was in that apartment for some time."

"Well, of course, Mr. Mason, finding a latent fingerprint is something like finding game in the woods. There may be lots of game but it may be rather difficult to find. It is necessary that the fingerprint be placed on a surface that will retain the latent impression and it must be developed within a certain limit of time."

"What limit?"

"Well, there, of course," the witness said, "you get into a factor which is governed by a lot of variables. It depends on weather conditions, upon the degree of humidity, the nature of the substance on which the latent fingerprint is impressed. I would say in this case,

Mr. Mason, that I could assume that the fingerprints I found were made within a period of seventy-two hours."

"More than that?"

"I don't think so, Mr. Mason. I am, of course, making an estimate, but under the circumstances I would say within a period of seventy-two hours."

"So that your examination indicated that the defendant had been in that apartment some time within seventy-two hours prior to the time your search was made?"

"Yes, sir."

"That I had been there within seventy-two hours prior to the time your search was made?"

"Yes, sir."

"Did you find fingerprints of Sylvia Atwood, the defendant's sister?"

"Yes, sir."

"So that she had been in the apartment some time within seventy-two hours prior to the time the fingerprints were developed?"

"Yes, sir."

"Did you find fingerprints of the decedent, J.J. Fritch?"

"Yes, sir."

"Many of them?"

"Quite a few."

"So he had been in the apartment within seventy-two hours of the time of your examination?"

"Yes, sir."

"And did you find fingerprints of George Brogan?"

"Naturally."

"So he had been in the apartment within seventy-two hours of the time the search was made?"

"Yes, sir."

"Now then," Mason said, "will you kindly tell us whether you found the fingerprints of Sergeant Holcomb of the Homicide Squad in that apartment?"

Haswell grinned. "As it happened," he said, "I did."

"So Sergeant Holcomb had been in that apartment within seventy-two hours of the time your search was made?"

"Yes, sir."

"Now then," Mason said, "can you kindly tell us whether there was anything in your examination that indicated whether Sergeant Holcomb had been in that apartment *before the murder was committed?*"

"No, sir. I only know I found his fingerprints."

"Do you know whether the defendant was in that apartment prior to the time the murder was committed?"

"No, sir. I only know that I found her fingerprints."

"Do you know that I was in the apartment prior to the time the murder was committed?"

"I only know that I found your fingerprints."

"So as far as your testimony is concerned," Mason said, "and let's be perfectly fair about this, I am talking now only about your testimony, there is no more reason to think that the defendant in this case committed the murder than that I committed the murder or that Sergeant Holcomb committed the murder?"

"Well, of course," the witness said, "I can't—"

"Oh, I'm going to object to that question as argumentative," Moon said. "Not proper cross-examination."

"Well, of course," the Court observed, "it *is* somewhat argumentative. However, Counsel is merely trying to point out the application of the time element. I think I will permit it."

"What's your answer?" Mason asked.

"The answer is no," the witness said. "I can't tell when those prints were made. I only know that within some time during which those prints could be preserved the defendant had been in that apartment."

"And that I had been in that apartment?"

"Yes, sir."

"And that Sergeant Holcomb had been in that apartment?"

"Yes, sir."

"And as far as anything your investigations disclosed there's just as much reason to believe that Sergeant Holcomb had been in that apartment and committed that murder as there is to believe that the defendant had been in that apartment and committed that murder?"

"Well, of course," the witness said, "I know that Sergeant Holcomb was in the apartment after the murder was committed."

"Do you know whether he was in the apartment before the murder was committed?"

"No, sir."

"Do you know whether the defendant was in that apartment after the murder was committed?"

"I understand that—well, now, wait a minute, if I have to answer that question fairly I will have to answer that I do not."

"Thank you," Mason said. "That's all."

Moon hesitated as though debating whether to ask another question, then decided against it and said, "That's all."

"Now then, Your Honor," Moon said, "I wish to call George Brogan once more, this time to direct his testimony to an entirely different phase of the case. This, if the Court please, is laying the foundation for the introduction in evidence of the spool of tape recording which has been the subject of previous examination and which spool was found by the police under a search warrant."

Brogan once more took the stand. His manner indicated that he knew he was facing an ordeal which was far from welcome.

"Now, Mr. Brogan," Moon said, "I am going to ask you if prior to the seventh of this month you had had occasion to converse with Perry Mason?"

"I had. Yes, sir."

"And where did that conversation take place?"

"In my apartment."

"And did that conversation have something to do with any of the Bain family?"

"It did. Yes, sir. It affected property rights, which, in turn, were important to each member of the family, that is, potentially important."

"And did those conversations have to do with the activities of Mr. J.J. Fritch, the man who was murdered?"

"They did. Yes, sir."

"Can you describe them generally? You don't need to go into detail, but tell what was the general nature of the conversation and the negotiations."

Brogan took a long breath, shifted his position once more, hesitated, seeking to choose his words.

Judge Kaylor glanced at Mason, then turned to Moon. "Isn't this somewhat remote?"

"No, Your Honor. It proves motive and it is laying the foundation for the introduction of this evidence which was discussed earlier, a spool of recorded tape, which the police found *in the possession of Mr. Perry Mason.*"

"Is there any objection?" Judge Kaylor asked, glancing at Mason, who sat completely relaxed, sliding his thumb and forefinger up and down the polished sides of a pencil.

"None whatever," Mason said, smiling affably.

"Very well, go ahead," Judge Kaylor said. "I would suggest, however, that we be as brief as possible. I think that if Counsel wishes to prove motivation this witness can testify generally to the facts in connection with the business negotiations and not go into a lot of detail."

"You have heard what the Court said," Moon said to the witness. "Just be brief. Tell us generally what this discussion was about."

Brogan said, "I happened to find out that Mr. Fritch was involved in a matter which he had effectively concealed for many years. He claimed that there had been some connection between him and Ned Bain, the father of the defendant. If that connection had been established it might well have resulted in a great property loss so far as the Bain family was concerned."

"So what did you do?"

"I felt that I might be able to be of some value and offered my services to the Bains."

"All of the Bains?"

"No, a representative of the Bain family."

"Who?"

"Mrs. Sylvia Atwood."

"By Mrs. Atwood you are referring to the sister of the defendant?"

"Yes, sir."

"And what happened?"

"Mrs. Atwood retained Mr. Mason. Mr. Mason called on me and I tried to make my position clear, that I was under the circumstances in a position to act somewhat in the nature of intermediary, but that if I were to do so I wanted it definitely understood that I was representing the Bain family and no one else, that under no circumstances did I wish to affiliate myself with Mr. Fritch."

"May I ask why you adopted that attitude?"

"For ethical reasons. It was a matter of business ethics."

"Was there perhaps something unethical about Mr. Fritch's approach?"

"I felt there was."

"What did you feel was unethical about it?"

"Frankly, I felt it was plain blackmail."

"And you didn't wish any part of that?"

"Definitely not."

"But you did approach Mrs. Atwood?"

"Yes, sir."

"And she in turn retained Mr. Mason?"

"Yes, sir."

"Now was there a spool of tape recording which entered into those negotiations?"

"Yes, sir."

"What was the nature of that recording?"

"It purported to be a recording of a conversation which had taken place between Mr. Fritch and Mr. Ned Bain, the father of the defendant."

"And what happened?"

"Mr. Mason and Mrs. Atwood came to my apartment. They wanted to hear that recorded conversation. I played it for them."

"How did you come to have possession of it?"

"Mr. Fritch gave it to me for that purpose. He thought that it would best serve his own interests to have Mr. Mason and Mrs. Atwood acquainted with the details of his claim, and as soon as he knew Mr. Mason had been retained he knew he was going to have to make out a strong case if he was going to get any money. He knew he had to put all his facts on the table."

"And what happened?"

"I had assured Mr. Fritch that while I would not represent him in any way I would stake my reputation on the fact that nothing would happen to that tape recording."

"Did something happen to it?"

"It did."

"What?"

"It was ruined."

"How?"

"I don't know how. I certainly wish I did. I gather, however, that it was some form of a radio-active polarization brought about by a clever subterfuge on the part of Mr. Mason."

"In what way?"

Judge Kaylor glanced at Mason. "Surely," he said, "we are now entering a field of surmise and something that seems to me to be definitely outside the issues in this case."

"If the Court please, it is showing the motivation," Moon explained, "and it is also laying the foundations for the introduction of this spool of tape recording in evidence."

"Well, there seems to be no objection," Judge Kaylor said. "Proceed. Answer the question."

"I don't know how Mr. Mason did it," Brogan said. "He had a device with him. He pretended it was a hearing aid. I don't know *what* it was. I am assuming that it was a polarizing device which enabled him to erase the recorded tape as it was being played."

"And what happened?"

"Mr. Mason asked me to play the tape back a second time. When I did there was nothing on it, the tape was completely blank."

"What did you do?"

"I assured Mr. Mason, of course, that I felt it must be something that was wrong with the machine, and stated that I wished time to have the machine fixed."

"Why did you state that it was something wrong with the machine?"

"I simply couldn't bear the thought of having something happen to that tape and have to face Mr. Fritch and confess to him that I had been outwitted in the matter. I knew that Mr. Fritch wouldn't accept that explanation, that he would be terribly angry."

"Now at that time did you think this recorded tape was the only tape recording of that conversation?"

"I did. Yes, sir."

"Did anything happen to change your mind?"

"It did. Yes, sir."

"What?"

"I was forced to report to Mr. Fritch what had happened. At that time I learned that the tape recording which I had, and which I assumed to be an original, which I may say Mr. Fritch had repeatedly assured me was the original and only tape recording, was, in fact, a dubbed copy of another master tape recording."

"And where was this master tape recording?"

"In the possession of Mr. Fritch."

"And what did Mr. Fritch tell you about it, if anything?"

"In the presence of the defendant or in the presence of Mr. Mason as Counsel for the defendant?" Judge Kaylor asked.

"Well, no, Your Honor. I am trying to show—"

"No objection, Your Honor. No objection whatever," Mason said. "Let him go into this to his heart's content."

"Well, of course, if there's no objection, the Court ordinarily permits evidence to go in. I am assuming that Counsel is familiar with facts that the Court does not know, and therefore there probably is some underlying connection here, but it seems to me that to expect this defendant to be bound by a conversation which took place between Mr. Fritch and this witness, and of which she presumably had no knowledge, is somewhat stretching a point."

"It's quite all right," Mason said.

"Very well," Judge Kaylor snapped. "Answer the question, Mr. Witness."

Brogan said, "Fritch reported to me that he had anticipated something might happen to the genuine recorded conversation which he had, and therefore he had given me a dubbed copy so that I could point out to Mrs. Atwood the position in which she found herself, while he had retained the original so that nothing *could* happen to it. He said that he would make me another copy."

"What was your reaction to this?"

"I was very much embarrassed because I had assured both Mr. Mason and Mrs. Atwood that this recording which I had was the original, and was the only one in existence, that I had Mr. Fritch's assurance that this was the case."

"But Mr. Fritch himself told you that he had another original recording?"

"He did. Yes, sir."

"Did you have occasion to see that recording?"

"I did. Yes, sir."

"Was there anything about it that was distinctive?"

"Yes, sir."

"What?"

"There were numerous splices in the tape itself, that is, indications that two or perhaps more pieces of tape had been spliced together."

"And did Mr. Fritch make another copy or another dubbed duplicate of that original?"

"Yes, sir."

"And what did you do?"

"I was very much disturbed because I realized I had been jockeyed into a perfectly untenable position."

"In what way?"

"If representatives of the Bain family had made any arrangements with Mr. Fritch to secure the dubbed copy, the original would still have been just as much of a menace as ever."

"I take it that there was something in the recorded conversation which you felt the Bain family would not care to have made public?"

"Yes, sir."

"And do you know from your own observations that Mr. Fritch did on the sixth of this month have the original, which you have referred to as having been spliced and showing evidences of having been spliced?"

"Yes, sir."

"And where was that?"

"In his apartment."

"Where did he keep it in his apartment?"

"I don't know. He went and got it for me and showed it to me. He also showed me a tape recorder on which he could make duplications."

"Now then, you had an appointment with Mr. Mason for nine o'clock on the morning of the seventh?"

"Yes, sir."

"And with Mrs. Atwood?"

"Yes, sir."

"Were you there at your apartment at nine o'clock?"

"Not at nine o'clock. No, sir."

"Will you kindly tell the Court just what you did?"

"Well, I was very much interested in trying to learn the reactions of Mr. Mason and Mrs. Atwood. I was particularly interested in trying to find out the method by which Mr. Mason, without ever having had his hands on that spool of tape recording, had managed to cause the conversation on that tape recording to vanish into thin air."

"So what did you do?"

"I had an engagement for a poker game on the evening of the sixth. I deliberately planned to stay all night at that poker game and to be about five or ten minutes late in getting to my apartment."

"Why did you do that?"

"I wanted to find out what Mr. Mason and Mrs. Atwood said about that tape recording. I wanted to know what their reactions were. I wanted to find out what their confidential thoughts were on the subject."

"So what did you do, if anything?"

"I deliberately planned to absent myself from my apartment. I left my door unlocked. I left a note pinned to the door in an envelope addressed to Mr. Perry Mason. That note told him that I was playing poker and it might be I would be delayed, that he was to enter my apartment and wait for me."

"What else did you do?"

"I planted a tape recorder with a hidden microphone."

"Where?"

"So that it would record any conversation which took place either in front of the door of the apartment or in the apartment itself."

"And did you make some arrangement to have that microphone turned on?"

"I did. Yes, sir."

"How? In what way?"

"By use of an electric clock."

"Can you explain that a little more fully?"

"There are clocks that are run by electricity. They keep accurate time. You can get an attachment on those clocks which is similar to an alarm. When a predetermined time comes that attachment will turn on an electric current, actuating any device that you want. I set this clock for eight-fifty, so that at ten minutes to nine the clock would automatically turn on a tape recorder and start it running. I left a thirty-minute spool of tape on there so that I could know everything that was said by persons who were standing in front of my door or who had entered my apartment. I left the transom open and the microphone was in the ceiling of the room just inside the transom."

"And how long would that recording device continue to operate?"

"Until twenty minutes past nine. It would start at eight-fifty. It was a thirty-minute spool. I expected to be there before nine-twenty. I expected to give them about five or ten minutes to indulge in conversation and then I would show up."

"Your absence therefore was deliberate?"

"Yes, sir."

"And did you show up?"

"Yes, sir."

"When?"

"About nine-five."

"And you found Mr. Mason there?"

"Mr. Mason, Mrs. Atwood and Mr. Mason's secretary, Miss Street, I believe her name is."

"And you entered the apartment?"

"Yes, sir."

"And what happened?"

"Then was when I discovered the body of J.J. Fritch."

"Now then, did you subsequently turn on that tape recorder to see what conversation had taken place?"

"I did. Yes, sir."

"I am going to ask you if there was anything in that conversation about a previous discovery of the body of J.J. Fritch."

"There was. Yes, sir."

"And were there any comments made by Mr. Mason in connection with that discovery?"

"Yes, sir."

"Advice?"

"Yes, sir."

"Did Mr. Mason say anything about searching for a spool of original tape recording which he was satisfied Mr. Fritch had?"

"Yes, sir. He did."

"Do you have that tape recording here?"

"Yes, sir."

"Is it possible to recognize the voices?"

"It is. Yes, sir."

"If the Court please," Moon said, "I wish at this time to introduce this tape recording. I have here a machine which will play that tape recording, and I think the Court will be interested in hearing it."

"Any objection?" Judge Kaylor asked.

"Lots of objection," Mason said. "This doesn't have anything to do with the crime. It doesn't bind the defendant, Hattie Bain, in any way. *She* wasn't present at that time. *She* didn't hear what was being said. Therefore she can't be bound by it."

"Her attorney was there," Moon said.

"At that time I wasn't her counsel," Mason pointed out. "You can't bind her by something I have said before I was retained to represent her. Otherwise you might as well go back ten years and find something I said."

"I think we're entitled to put this in evidence. It's highly significant," Moon commented.

"You may put it in evidence under certain circumstances," Mason said. "You would have to ask one of the persons present as to whether a certain conversation did not take place. If that person admitted that conversation that's all there is to it. Your tape recording can't be introduced. If the person denied that conversation you'd then be in a position to introduce the tape recording to impeach that person *provided* you could prove that the clock worked, that the tape recording actually was made covering the period between eight-fifty and nine-twenty, and, further, that one of the voices on the tape recording was recognizable by anyone as the voice of the party whom you sought to impeach. Even then the recording would be evidence only of impeaching circumstances and not of a fact."

"I think that's the law," Judge Kaylor said.

"Oh, if the Court please," Moon said angrily. "I expect to show by this tape recording that Mr. Mason himself, knowing that J.J. Fritch was dead, proceeded unlawfully to invade and enter the apartment of J.J. Fritch *for the specific purpose of illegally and unlawfully looking for this spliced tape recording.*"

"Therefore, you mean that I murdered Fritch?" Mason asked.

"You may ultimately become involved as an accessory," Moon snapped.

"Now what tape recording do you want to introduce?" Judge Kaylor asked.

"Right now the one made in front of Brogan's apartment, showing the discovery of the body and Mason's statement that he was going to make an illegal search."

"The objection to that is sustained," Judge Kaylor ruled. "None of the participants in that conversation are being tried in this case, nor is it claimed that conversation took place in the presence of the defendant."

"I also want to introduce the tape recording Brogan has testified to as being the Fritch original tape recording."

"You'll have to lay a foundation first."

"I thought I had done so, Your Honor."

"This witness has merely stated there was such a tape recording. He hasn't identified it."

"If the Court will listen to it, the Court will become convinced that the tape recording contains proof of its own authenticity. It lays its own foundation."

Judge Kaylor shook his head. "Some witness will have to identify it."

"Well, Brogan can state that this recording is similar in appearance to the one Fritch had."

"Look out of the window," Mason said. "You'll see a thousand automobiles in the parking lot below. They all of them are 'similar in appearance.' You'll find some that are identical models. If you're going to identify them you're going to have to get into individual characteristics rather than overall group characteristics."

"You don't need to tell me how to practice law!" Moon flared angrily.

"Someone does," Mason said, and sat down.

Judge Kaylor said, "That will do, Counselor. The Court does not wish to have any sarcastic personal interchanges between Counsel."

"I was merely replying in kind," Mason said.

"Well, I don't want Counsel to reply in kind. I want this hearing kept on an orderly plane. Now then, gentlemen, I have listened patiently to this line of testimony. I think some witness will have to identify that tape recording if it's to be introduced. I suggest you pass this phase of the case for the present."

"That's all for now, Mr. Brogan," Moon said. "I'll recall you after you've listened to this tape recording.

Brogan got up to leave the stand.

Mason said, "I want to cross-examine."

"Go ahead, Mr. Mason," Judge Kaylor said.

Perry Mason arose from his chair, walked around the end of the counsel table and stood waiting for Brogan to look at him.

Brogan glanced up quickly, saw Mason's hard eyes, features which might have been carved from granite, and hastily averted his glance.

The silence became significant.

"Proceed," Judge Kaylor said.

"Did you understand that Fritch had robbed a bank?" Mason asked.

"I gathered there was a possibility that had been the case."

"Did you know him at the time of the bank robbery?"

"I—I think I did."

"Did you know how much Fritch wanted in return for his silence about the details of that bank robbery?"

"I knew he wanted a substantial sum of money."

"You were willing to act as intermediary and negotiate for the payment of that sum of money?"

"Not in the sense your question implies."

"How then?"

"I was willing to do what I could to help Mr. Bain—the Bain family."

"Did you know the Bains?"

"Not personally."

"Why were you so willing to help them?"

"Because I thought they were being—well, I thought they needed—"

"You started to say you thought they were being blackmailed, didn't you?"

"Yes."

"They were being blackmailed, weren't they?"

"Well, it depends. It was rather a peculiar situation taken by and large."

"And you were willing to participate in that blackmail?"

"No, sir."

"You were willing to collect the money from them and turn it over to Fritch?"

"Well that, of course, is a bald statement. That excludes my motives, which, I think, were rather laudable."

"Just answer the question," Mason said. "You were willing to collect money from them and turn it over to Fritch?"

"Well, yes, if you want it that way."

"In a blackmail proposition?"

"I thought it amounted to blackmail."

"You gathered that Fritch was in a position to give certain information to the bank which would make it appear that money which had been stolen from the bank had been used by Mr. Bain to purchase property which subsequently became very valuable through the development of oil, and that Mr. Bain had used this money with the knowledge that it represented the loot taken in a bank robbery. Is that correct?"

"That's substantially correct."

"Now then, during the night when the murder was committed you were not in your apartment?"

"That is right."

"You were intimately acquainted with Mr. Fritch?"

"I was in a way co-operating with him. Mr. Fritch wanted money. He thought I was in a position to get it for him."

"And you were trying to get money for him?"

"I was trying to get the matter cleaned up."

"By getting it cleaned up you mean getting the Bain family to put up enough money to buy the silence of J.J. Fritch?"

"Well—to get it cleaned up."

"Fritch had an apartment right across from yours?"

"Yes, sir."

"Who secured that apartment for him?"

"I did."

"Now Fritch anticipated that he might have to remain out of circulation for a considerable period of time, did he not?"

"I can't tell you what was in Mr. Fritch's mind."

"Didn't he so communicate to you?"

The witness hesitated, said, "Well, I believe that at one time he did say something like that."

"You went into Fritch's apartment from time to time?"

"Yes, sir."

"And he went into your apartment?"

"Yes, sir."

"He had a key to your apartment?"

"Well—"

"Did he or didn't he?"

"Well, yes, he did."

"You had a key to his apartment?"

"He asked me to—"

"Did you have a key to his apartment?"

"Yes, sir."

"You were in there from time to time?"

"Yes, sir."

"Were you familiar with the preparations he had made to keep himself in a place of concealment in the event it became necessary?"

"Just what do you mean by that?"

"Specifically, were you aware of the fact that he had purchased a very large deep-freeze box, that he had stocked that with all sorts of provisions so that in case of necessity it wouldn't be necessary for him to go out for anything, that he wouldn't have to be seen in public, on the street, or even in the elevator of the building?"

"Yes, sir."

"Do you know what that deep-freeze unit cost?"

"Around seven hundred dollars I believe."

"And it was stocked with provisions worth a good deal of money?"

"I believe so."

"More than a hundred dollars?"

"I believe so."

"More than two hundred dollars?"

"I believe around—well, around three hundred or three hundred and twenty-five dollars."

"Who put up the money for that?"

Brogan squirmed. "Of course, I was in a peculiar position and—"

"Did you put up the money which represented the purchase price of the deep-freeze icebox and the material that was in it, the foodstuffs?"

"I loaned Mr. Fritch a certain sum of money."

"How much?"

"Two thousand dollars."

"And do you know that that money, or a good part of it, went toward defraying the expense of moving into that apartment, of installing a television set and purchasing the deepfreeze icebox and the provisions that were in that deep-freeze icebox?"

"I surmised that it did. Yes, sir."

"So by the time we divorce your efforts of all of the protestations of ethical integrity with which you have sought to surround yourself, the fact remains that you financed J.J. Fritch in his blackmailing activities?"

"I don't so regard it."

"You 'grubstaked' him?"

"I do not so regard it."

"I do," Mason said.

"Well, you're entitled to your opinion," Brogan said. "I'm entitled to mine."

"Now then," Mason said, "on the night of the murder you *deliberately* stayed away?"

"Yes, sir."

"You were in a poker game?"

"Yes, sir."

"You can prove where you were every minute of the time?"

"Absolutely every minute of the time up until approximately eight-twenty."

"Where were you after eight-twenty?"

"I stopped in for a bite to eat. Frankly, I don't even remember the restaurant. It was some restaurant that caught my eye as I was driving along the street. It happened to be open. I looked in and there were vacant tables and an efficient-looking waitress was standing apparently with nothing to do, so I felt I could get some breakfast without too much delay. I stopped in for some hot coffee and something to eat."

"You had been engaged in playing poker all night, that is, all the night of the sixth and all the morning of the seventh up until eight-twenty?"

"Yes, sir."

"With how many people?"

"There were seven people in the game, and every one of them can and will vouch for the fact that I was there all night."

"You had arranged this poker game deliberately?"

"No, sir. I—well, perhaps I did have something to do with arranging it."

"Then you did it deliberately so you would have a legitimate excuse for being away from the apartment, so that you in turn could leave a note on the door and use this tape recorder in order to learn what Mrs. Atwood and I were talking about?"

"Perhaps so. I could have had several motives."

"But that was one of them?"

"Yes."

"Primarily you wanted to know whether we were going to pay Fritch money for the recording?"

"I was *primarily* interested in seeing how you had managed to erase the voice recording on that tape without going near it."

"But you did deliberately arrange to be absent during the period the murder was to be committed?"

"Yes, sir. I—now wait a minute, wait a minute! I didn't mean that."

"Then why did you say it?"

"You said it. You put the words in my mouth."

"You gave yourself an alibi, didn't you?"

"I had a perfect alibi, Mr. Mason. You can't involve me in that murder no matter what you do."

"Why not?"

"Because the murder was committed while I was seated in the presence of seven witnesses."

"You left the poker game in order to get some money, didn't you?"

"That's right."

"When was that?"

"At about five in the morning. I was only gone for approximately twenty minutes."

"Where did you go?"

"To see a friend."

"What friend?"

"I don't care to tell."

"Why not?"

"It might embarrass him."

"What did you do?"

"I got fifteen hundred dollars."

"And what time was that?"

"Five in the morning, Mr. Mason," Brogan said angrily. "Two hours after the extreme limit that the doctor says J.J. Fritch must have been killed."

"How far," Mason asked, "was it from your apartment to the place where the poker game was in progress?"

"Approximately—oh, I don't know, five blocks."

"You could have driven it in a car in five minutes?"

"I suppose so. If I weren't tied up in traffic."

"There wasn't any traffic to tie you up at five o'clock in the morning?"

"No," Brogan said sarcastically, "I could have driven from that poker game to my apartment at five o'clock in the morning. I could have been there at five minutes past five. I could have stayed there until fifteen minutes past five. I could then have returned to my poker game at five-twenty. Now then, Mr. Mason, suppose you figure out how I could have possibly committed a murder that was committed between midnight and three o'clock in the morning by leaving a poker game at five o'clock. I have never yet been able to turn back the hands of the clock."

Judge Kaylor said with some annoyance, "The witness will refrain from asking Counsel questions, the witness will refrain from challenging Counsel, the witness will confine himself to answering questions."

Mason said, "As a matter of fact, Your Honor, if the Court will bear with us I appreciate that question very much. I would like to answer it."

Judge Kaylor glanced at Mason as though he could hardly believe his ears.

"As a matter of fact," Mason said, "the solution is very simple. All he had to do was to drive to his apartment, stab J.J. Fritch with the ice pick, take all of the frozen food out of the big deep-freeze icebox, dump Fritch's body in on its back with the knees and the elbows bent, close the lid and return to his poker game, stay there until eight-twenty, then dash up to his apartment, pull Fritch out of the deep-freeze unit, put him in his liquor closet, dump the food back into the food container, walk around the block, wait until nine o'clock, come hurrying up to his apartment and state that he had been at breakfast. The facts would then match the facts which we have in this case. The temperature would have been so tampered with that the autopsy surgeon would have been fooled into believing that death had taken place at somewhere around one o'clock in the morning, instead of four hours later."

Mason walked back, sat down at the counsel table, tilted back in his swivel chair and smiled.

Judge Kaylor, leaning forward, glanced goggle-eyed from the witness to Mason, then to the deputy district attorney.

"That's a lie!" George Brogan shouted. "I never did anything of the sort!"

"We object to Counsel's statement. It's not evidence. It's not even logical," Moon yelled at the judge.

"Show me where it isn't logical," Mason said.

The courtroom broke into such an uproar that it took the bailiff several seconds to pound it back into any semblance of silence.

"Do you have any vestige of proof for this astounding accusation, Mr. Mason?"

"It's not an accusation," Mason said. "The witness merely asked me a question. He challenged me to show how he could have committed the murder, and I answered that challenge."

"It couldn't have been done that way," Moon assured the Court.

"Why not?"

"The doctor wouldn't have been fooled by any such an expedient."

"Call him back on the stand and ask him," Mason challenged.

There was an awkward interval of silence.

"Are there any further questions of this witness?" Judge Kaylor asked somewhat lamely.

"One or two more," Mason said.

"Very well, proceed," Judge Kaylor ordered, but it was quite apparent that he was engaged in deep thought.

Mason said, "You knew that Fritch had robbed a bank some years ago?"

"I knew he was supposed to have done so."

"And that the amount of the loot had been approximately two hundred thousand dollars?"

"So I understood."

"Fritch was not alone in that robbery?"

"I don't know."

"You knew that the reports mentioned that he wasn't alone?"

"So I understand. He had a confederate, perhaps two. I don't know."

Mason said, so casually that for a moment the full import of his question failed to dawn on the spectators, "Now, Mr. Brogan, were you one of the men who participated in that robbery?"

Brogan started to get up out of the witness chair, then sank back down into it.

There was a long interval of silence in the courtroom.

"Oh, if the Court please," Moon said, "this question is insulting. It is without any foundation of fact. It is simply a shot in the dark. It is asked only for the purpose of embarrassing and humiliating the witness."

"Let him answer it then," Mason said. "Let him declare under oath that he wasn't one of the members of that holdup gang. The crime itself has been outlawed, but if he now says under oath that he wasn't a member of the gang he can be prosecuted for perjury."

Again there was an interval of silence.

"I object to the question," Moon said. "It's—"

"Overruled," Judge Kaylor snapped.

The judge glared down at the unhappy witness. "You heard that question?" he asked.

"Yes, sir."

"You understand that question?"

"Yes, sir."

"Answer it."

Brogan shifted his position, glanced at the ceiling, said, "I don't think I care to answer it."

"The Court orders you to answer it."

Brogan shook his head. "I'm not going to answer it."

"On what ground?" Mason asked, smiling.

"On the ground that the answer might incriminate me."

Mason grinned at the discomfited deputy district attorney, then turned back to Brogan.

"You were losing in the poker game, Mr. Brogan?" Mason asked.

"I've already told you I was."

"And at five o'clock you went out to get more money?"

"Yes, sir."

"And returned with a considerable sum of cash?"

"Yes, sir."

"And you can't tell us where you secured this cash?"

"I told you I got it from a friend."

"And you refuse to divulge the name of the friend?"

"That's right."

"Why?"

"On the ground—I don't think I have to."

"I think it's incompetent, irrelevant and immaterial and not proper cross-examination," Moon said.

Mason grinned and said to Judge Kaylor, "Order him to answer the question and he'll refuse to answer *that* one on the ground the answer will incriminate him."

"I object," Moon said. "I don't feel this is proper cross-examination."

Judge Kaylor, watching the witness carefully, said, "I'm going to overrule the objection. Answer the question."

Brogan doggedly shook his head.

"Are you going to answer that question?" Mason asked.

"No, sir."

"Why not?"

"On the same ground, Mr. Mason, you mentioned, that the answer might incriminate me."

Mason said, "As a matter of fact, the friend from whom you secured this money was a close, intimate friend, was it not?"

"Yes, sir."

"A very close friend?"

"Yes, sir."

"Perhaps the closest friend you have?"

"Perhaps."

"In other words," Mason said, "you got that money from yourself. *You* were the friend. You left the poker game and went to your apartment in order to get cash out of the secret wall safe in that apartment, didn't you?"

Brogan fidgeted.

"Answer the question," Judge Kaylor snapped.

Brogan looked at the judge appealingly. "Can't you see, Your Honor, he's just driving me into a position here where he's going to pin this murder on me no matter what happens. I can't combat that kind of stuff."

"You can answer questions," Judge Kaylor said. "If you went to your apartment at that time in order to get money you can say so."

"I don't have to say so," Brogan said. "I refuse to answer."

"On what ground?"

"On the ground that it will incriminate me."

Mason grinned. "That's all," he said. "No more questions. That's all, Mr. Brogan."

"That's all, Mr. Brogan. Leave the stand," Moon instructed.

His face red with anger, Moon said, "If the Court please, insinuations are not proof. Innuendoes are certainly not entitled to the weight of evidence.

"I know, however, *why* they were made and I think the Court knows why they were made. I intend to prevent the garbled reports which I am satisfied Counsel hoped would find their way into the press. I am going to recall Dr. Hanover and spike these rumors immediately and at once."

"Very well, call him," Mason said.

Mason stood up and beckoned to Della Street, who was seated near the back of the courtroom.

Della left the courtroom and shortly returned carrying an armful of books. She placed them on the table in front of Mason, withdrew from the courtroom and a moment later returned carrying another armful of books.

Dr. Hanover, taking the stand, looked down at the array of books which Mason had arranged so that the titles stamped in gilt on the backs of the books were visible to the witness on the stand.

"Now then," Moon said, "I'm going to ask Dr. Hanover a question. Doctor, would it have been possible for the conditions which you found when you examined that body to have been artificially induced by the body having been stored in a deep-freeze unit? In other words, is it at all possible that J.J. Fritch could have been murdered at five o'clock in the morning, the body kept for an interval of some two or three hours in a deep-freeze icebox, so that you would have placed the time of death at between midnight and 3:00 A.M.?"

"Just a moment," Mason said. "Before you answer that question, Doctor, I want to object on the ground that no proper foundation has been laid."

"I have already shown the doctor's qualifications," Moon said.

"I'd like to cross-examine him purely in regard to his qualifications," Mason announced.

"Very well," Judge Kaylor ruled. "That is your privilege."

Mason picked up a book. "Have you ever heard of a book entitled *Homicide Investigation* by Dr. LeMoyne Snyder, Doctor?"

"Yes, sir."

"What is the reputation of that book?"

"Excellent."

"It is a standard authority in the field of forensic medicine?"

"It is."

"Have you ever heard of Professor Glaister's book *Forensic Medicine and Toxicology?*"

"Indeed yes."

"What is its reputation?"

"Excellent."

"It is a standard authority in the field of forensic medicine?"

"It is."

Mason started opening the books to pages which had been marked with bookmarks. Dr. Hanover's fascinated gaze followed the lawyer's activity as he spread the books open, piled one on top of the other until he had an imposing array.

"Now then," Mason said, "I am going to object to the question asked by Counsel on the ground that no proper foundation has been laid, that it assumes facts not in evidence, that it fails to state facts which are in evidence."

"What facts are omitted?" Moon challenged.

"Mainly the fact that Dr. Hanover based his testimony in part upon the state of the contents of the stomach and the condition of the meal which he *assumed* had been ingested at the usual meal hour. I am going to point out that Dr. Hanover has no means of knowing when that meal was ingested and therefore his testimony is dependent entirely upon that of body temperature.

"I also want to point out that the witness, Mrs. Lorton, your own witness, by whose testimony you are bound, stated specifically that when the defendant went to the apartment of J.J. Fritch, whom she knew as Frank Reedy, that Mr. J.J. Fritch opened the door and let her in. She didn't say 'some man.' She said that *Fritch* himself opened the door and let her in. Now at that time it is quite apparent that Fritch must have been fully dressed. If the witness Lorton saw him clearly enough to know that he was the one who let the defendant into the apartment, she would certainly have noticed if Mr. Fritch had answered the door in his underwear and admitted a woman to his apartment while he was so attired. It is, therefore, obvious that the only yardstick which Dr. Hanover has for fixing the time of death is that of temperature, and since it now appears in the evidence that Fritch was apparently fully dressed at the time of Miss Bain's call, but was clad in his underwear at the time he met his death, I submit that the witness be not permitted to answer this question as it is now asked."

"Oh, I'll put it to him this way," Moon said. "I'll meet the issue head-on. I'll take the bull by the horns. Dr. Hanover, assuming only the facts that you yourself know, assuming that you don't know the time Fritch ingested the meal which you found in his stomach, predicating your testimony entirely on the temperature of the body, is it or is it not possible that the decedent met his death later than three o'clock in the morning, but the conditions of temperature which you found could have been caused by placing the body in a deep-freeze compartment?"

"Also pointing out," Mason interjected, "the fact that this would absolutely account for the position of the hands at the time that *rigor mortis* of the arms and shoulders set in."

"I don't have to put that in my question," Moon said, testily.

Mason grinned. "I'm merely calling it to the doctor's attention because his professional reputation is at stake, and I may also point out to the witness and to Counsel that before we get done we're going to *prove* what actually happened."

"You don't need to threaten this witness," Moon shouted.

"I'm not threatening him, I'm cautioning him," Mason said, and sat down.

"Answer the question," Moon said.

Dr. Hanover ran his hand over his bald head, glanced once more at the books Mason had opened, said to the deputy district attorney, "That is, of course, rather a difficult question."

"What's difficult about it?"

"I have previously observed," Dr. Hanover said, "that in fixing the time of death from the temperature of the body, it is necessary to take into consideration the manner in which the body is clothed and the temperature of the surrounding environment. When I fixed the time of death as being between twelve o'clock and 3:00 A.M., I took into consideration the fact that the body was unclothed save for an athletic undershirt and boxer trunks. I also took into consideration the temperature of the apartment in which the body was found."

The doctor squirmed uneasily. "I will have to say that if you change any of those constant factors, or factors which I took to be constant, you naturally change my conclusions."

"But would that change your conclusions enough so that it would make that much of a time difference?" Moon protested.

Dr. Hanover, now having the deputy district attorney on the defensive, said quietly, "I'm afraid you would have to tell me, Mr. Moon, what was the temperature of the interior of that frozen-food container."

"I don't know," Moon said.

"Then I can't answer the question," Dr. Hanover said, smiling affably as he realized the avenue of escape he had opened up for himself.

"But we can find out," Moon said. "I suggest, if the Court please, that before there is any opportunity to tamper with the evidence in this case, the Court takes a look at the premises, that the Court adjourn so we can take a look at that icebox right here and now, and I suggest that the witness, Dr. Hanover, be required to go to inspect the premises with us."

"I think the Court would like to take a look at those premises," Judge Kaylor ruled. "Under the circumstances it would certainly seem to be advisable."

"Now just a moment, Your Honor," Moon went on. "I suggest that all of this grandstand divertissement has been done for the purpose of staving off the evil moment when Mr. Perry Mason has to account for how he came to have this master record with its splices and its background of murder. I suggest that all of this is a desperate expedient to draw a series of red herrings across the trail so that no one will examine him as to what he did when he entered Fritch's apartment at nine o'clock on the morning of the seventh. We have a tape recording of Mr. Mason's own voice showing that he himself went into Fritch's apartment for the purpose of making a search. I would like to have the Court hear that recording before we go out there."

Mason laughed. "The recording is completely, absolutely incompetent, irrelevant and immaterial. He can only use it for the purpose of impeaching me. He can't impeach me until I have testified to something that is opposed to the matters on that recording."

"Well, let me ask you," Moon said, "did you or didn't you enter Fritch's apartment at nine o'clock on the morning of the seventh?"

"Now, let's see," Mason said, "how long was that after the murder had been committed? Four hours or six hours?"

"That was at least six hours after the latest date the murder could have been committed!" Moon shouted. "That's what Dr. Hanover said and I'm sticking by his testimony until he changes it."

"I thought he'd changed it," Mason said. "However, you are now seeking to bind the defendant by some action I took six hours after the murder with which she is charged was committed, at a time when I have assured you I was not representing the defendant in this case. You are seeking to impeach me by introducing a tape recording of a conversation about which the defendant never knew, a conversation which took place in her absence."

Judge Kaylor shook his head. "I am afraid, Mr. Moon," he said, "that the objection is only too well taken. If, of course, you wish to use this tape recording for the purpose of substantiating a charge of unprofessional conduct, of concealing evidence, of becoming an accessory after the fact, or any other thing along those lines, you're entitled to do so, but you certainly can't use it here save for purposes of impeachment, and you can only impeach an answer of a witness that is made in response to a relevant question."

"So," Mason said, grinning, "I suggest we go look at the premises."

Judge Kaylor nodded. "Court will adjourn to reconvene at the premises in question."

The sound of the bailiff's gavel was the trigger which released a terrific uproar, a veritable pandemonium of voices as people engaged in arguments among themselves, called out comments to the various parties, some of them pressing forward to shake Mason's hand.

Hattie Bain glanced at Mason with wide, apprehensive eyes. "Is it—what does this mean—good or bad?"

"You'll have to be patient," Mason told her. "You're going to have to return to the custody of the matron."

"For how long?"

Mason grinned. "Not too long, the way things look now," he reassured her.

CHAPTER 15

Sergeant Holcomb unlocked the door of the Fritch apartment. His face was dark with anger.

"Now, of course," Judge Kaylor said, "it is usual in such cases to have all testimony taken in court and no testimony given while we are inspecting the premises. However, in this case since there is no jury I see no reason for enforcing such a rule.

"Now, Mr. Mason, you had reference to a deep-freeze box."

Mason nodded.

"Will you show me that, Sergeant?" Judge Kaylor asked.

Sergeant Holcomb led the way to the deep-freeze and threw back the cover.

"Now, as I understand it, Mr. Mason," Judge Kaylor said, "it is your contention that the body was placed in this deepfreeze."

"The Court will notice that the box is big enough to accommodate a man," Mason said.

"So are a thousand other iceboxes within a radius of a hundred yards," Sergeant Holcomb blurted.

"That will do, Sergeant," Judge Kaylor said. "I simply want to get Mr. Mason's contention. Now, Mr. Mason, is there any evidence, any single bit of evidence whatever that would indicate that the body had been put in here? There is the opportunity. The box is deep enough. However, you're going to have to show more than opportunity."

"In the first place," Mason said, "let's look at this."

He grabbed a pasteboard container of ice cream from the top of the deep-freeze, pulled the cover back, walked over to a silverware drawer in the cupboard, took out a teaspoon and plunged it down into the contents of the ice cream.

"Do you see what I mean?" he asked.

Judge Kaylor frowned. "I'm not certain that I do."

"This ice cream," Mason said, "was melted and then refrozen. See how it has frozen into crystals? It isn't smooth, as would have been the case if it had been stored without having been melted."

"I see, I see," Judge Kaylor said, his voice showing great interest. "Let me take a look at that."

He took the spoon and plunged it into the ice cream. The edge of the spoon rasped on frozen crystals.

"You see there's been a shrinkage in volume and it has frozen in the form of flakes, not as a smooth mixture," Mason said.

"Sergeant," Judge Kaylor snapped, his tone showing sudden interest, "open up another one of those ice-cream cartons."

Sergeant Holcomb pulled back the cover of another.

"The same condition," Mason said.

Judge Kaylor tested it with the spoon.

"Try another one, Sergeant."

Again Sergeant Holcomb took out another container, and Judge Kaylor plunged the spoon into it, brought up the contents so he could inspect them.

"This certainly is interesting," he said." Quite apparently this ice cream has been melted and refrozen."

"Any icebox is apt to have trouble," Sergeant Holcomb said. "I'm not certain but what we shut off this icebox when we were inspecting the place."

"Did you?" Judge Kaylor asked.

"I'm not certain."

"Well, you *should* be certain if you shut it off," the judge snapped.

He turned to Mason and there was a new interest in his voice. "Do you have any other evidence, Mr. Mason?"

"Certainly," Mason said. "Take out the packages. Test the bottom of the deep-freeze for blood stains."

"This is only a grandstand," Moon said. "This was done to get newspaper publicity to divert attention from—"

"Sergeant," Judge Kaylor asked, "did you remove the foodstuffs from this deep-freeze unit when you inspected the premises?"

"We didn't touch a thing in there," Sergeant Holcomb said. "We preserved everything just like it was. We looked the place over for fingerprints, that's all."

"Take them out," Judge Kaylor ordered.

"Of course, if we once take them out they'll start melting and Perry Mason will claim—"

"Take them out," Judge Kaylor ordered. "We've already ascertained that the ice cream has been out long enough to at least partially melt. Now get the rest of these things out. Let's look at the bottom of this box."

Sergeant Holcomb started lifting out the packages. He tossed out one package after another, piling them helterskelter on the floor, mixing up meats, frozen vegetables, frozen fruits. His manner was all but openly defiant.

As he neared the bottom of the box Judge Kaylor leaned over to look.

As the last package thudded to the floor, Judge Kaylor said, "It took you two minutes and eighteen seconds, Sergeant and—what's that?"

"That's a place where some of the juice leaked out of the meat," Holcomb said.

"Juice doesn't leak out of meat that's frozen hard," Judge Kaylor snapped. "I Want—Where's Dr. Hanover?"

"He's coming," Moon said. "He—"

"Well, get him," Judge Kaylor said. "I want every precaution taken to see that that stain is not disturbed. I want the police technicians up here. I want to find out if that's human blood. If there's enough of it to type I want the blood typed with that of the victim, J.J. Fritch."

Judge Kaylor turned to Mason. "How did you know that stain was there, Mr. Mason?" he asked.

"I didn't know, Your Honor. I surmised."

"Well, you took a long gamble on it," Judge Kaylor said, his manner suspicious.

Mason grinned at him. "What else was there to take a gamble on?" he asked.

Judge Kaylor thought that over and slowly a smile touched the corners of his stern mouth. "I guess you have something there, Counselor," he said, and turned away.

"Moreover," Mason pointed out, indicating the pile of packages which Sergeant Holcomb had dumped on the floor, "you'll notice a couple of blood smears on the outside of one of those packages. I think if Your Honor will have the fingerprint expert up here you may find there's a latent fingerprint outlined in blood on that package."

"That's where the butcher wrapped it up," Sergeant Holcomb said. "That—"

"Let me see, let me see," Judge Kaylor announced. He peered down at the package, then abruptly straightened. "Everybody clear out of here," he said. "I want everybody out of this apartment. I want this place sealed up. I want the fingerprint expert and the police pathologist in here and then *I'm* going to tell them how *I* want this apartment searched for evidence."

The judge glowered at Sergeant Holcomb and, angered by the surly look on Holcomb's face, added, "And you may consider that a rebuke, Sergeant."

CHAPTER 16

Mason, Della Street and Paul Drake sat in Drake's office. From time to time Mason consulted his wrist watch.

"Gosh, it's taking them long enough," he said.

"Don't worry," Drake told him. "They're being thorough, that's all. Believe me, they're really going to go to town this time. Judge Kaylor is mad as a wet hen."

Mason got up from his chair and started impatiently pacing the floor.

"I don't see how you had the thing figured out," Drake said.

"I *didn't* have it figured out," Mason told him. "That's what bothers me. I had to take a gamble. But remember this, Sylvia Atwood is a shrewd, calculating individual, yet she could have been telling the truth about that corpse tumbling out of the closet where the liquor was kept, and falling to the floor. I heard her scream and we could hear the thud of the body falling.

"The streaks of post-mortem lividity were on the back. Therefore, the body must have been lying on its back, but the body couldn't have been lying on its back if it had been in the liquor closet as she said.

"Now why would anyone move the body? The only reason I could think of was that someone didn't want the body found in the place where it had been lying while the post-mortem lividity formed.

"That meant it was to the advantage of someone, presumably the murderer, to see that the body was found in a different place from where it had been lying.

"The body was clad only in underwear. There were no clothes belonging to J.J. Fritch in Brogan's apartment. Therefore, it is reasonable to suppose that Fritch was killed in his own apartment. He was probably getting ready for bed, or perhaps he had already gone to bed and—"

"But the bed was made. It hadn't been slept in," Drake said.

Mason grinned. "Anyone can make a bed."

"Go on," Drake said.

"If the body had been moved," Mason said, "and judging from the peculiar position of the body it must have been crowded into some small space—"

"It would have been crowded in a small space in the liquor closet," Drake pointed out.

"But in that event the post-mortem lividity would have been lower down and not around the back of the neck, and the arms would have been down."

"Yes, I guess that's so," Drake said.

"Therefore," Mason said, "we came to the unmistakable conclusion that the body had been moved. Now Hattie Bain couldn't have moved that body, not by herself. Neither could Sylvia Atwood. Moreover, moving the body wouldn't have done *them* any good. The person who moved that body must have moved it for a reason. The only reason I can think of was that he wanted to establish an alibi. He wanted to establish it by interfering with the normal rate of cooling of a dead body."

"Do you think Brogan had time enough to do all that?" Drake asked.

Mason said, "Let's look at it this way, Paul. *Somebody* moved that body. It was done for a definite purpose. The most logical assumption is that it was done to build up an alibi, therefore we are looking for someone who has an alibi between midnight and two or three o'clock in the morning, but who does *not* have an alibi for a later hour.

"It has to be someone who is strong enough to have picked up a body and moved it. It has to be someone whom J.J. Fritch would have received in his underwear. We *know* that someone made the bed and fixed up Fritch's apartment, probably in order to make it appear Fritch had been killed earlier before he had gone to bed."

"How do we know that?" Drake asked.

"Because," Mason said, "the body may have been put in an icebox. That would make the autopsy surgeon think the murder had been committed earlier than had been the case. But even the autopsy surgeon fixes the earliest date at midnight. Now when I went in there that morning *the television was on.* Fritch would hardly have had the television on much after midnight. There weren't any programs at that hour. That indicates Fritch either met his death before midnight or that somebody tampered with the evidence."

Drake nodded.

"And since Hattie saw him alive after midnight, it means someone tampered with the evidence."

"Yes, that's logical," Drake admitted.

"Now then," Mason went on, "one of the persons who fits the description of our hypothetical murderer is George Brogan, but there is one defect to our line of reasoning connecting him with the crime."

"What's that?"

"He had no motive."

"What do you mean, he had no motive? Wasn't Fritch sore at him and—?"

"Why should Fritch be sore at him? Brogan was getting money out of Bain for Fritch."

"But couldn't he have stolen that recording and—?"

"No," Mason said, "as soon as Fritch died the menace against the Bain estate was wiped out. The tape recording doesn't prove anything. It would only have been a means of corroborating Fritch's testimony. If Fritch had stated that Bain was his confederate and that Bain knew the money which went into that oil land had come from the bank, that would have been one thing. He could have used the tape recording to bolster his testimony, but without that testimony you certainly couldn't use the tape recording."

"By George," Drake said, "that's so!"

The telephone rang sharply.

Della Street jerked the receiver to her ear, said, "Yes. Hello, Mr. Mason's office. . . . Oh, just a minute.

"It's for you, Paul."

Drake picked up the receiver, said, "Hello. Yes. . . . The devil. . . . You're sure. . . . A good print. . . . The same type of blood. . . . Okay, thanks. Keep me posted."

He hung up the telephone, grinned at Mason and said, "You've hit a jackpot, Perry."

"How come?"

"They've made a test of the stains of blood on the bottom of the icebox. They're human blood. They're blood of the same type as that of J.J. Fritch. It's an unusual and rare type. Therefore, the similarity in typing is significant.

"They've found perfect latent fingerprints outlined in blood on the packages of food that were taken out of the deep-freeze container. There again the blood is the same type as that of J.J. Fritch. They've photographed the blood-stained prints but they can't match them with those of anyone in the case. They're not Sylvia Atwood's. They're not Hattie Bain's. They're not Ned Bain's. They're not yours. They're not George Brogan's."

Mason grinned and lit a cigarette.

"Any suggestions?" Drake asked.

"Lots of them."

"Such as what?"

Mason said, "Let's narrow down our line of reasoning, Paul. We need someone who had an alibi for the hours before the murder was committed but who could have no alibi afterward. We need someone who was strong enough to lift the body of J.J. Fritch. Moreover, we need someone who was scientific enough to realize that the question of body temperature would be considered by the autopsy surgeon as an element in determining the time of death.

"Furthermore, there's the question of motivation to be considered. We need someone who stood to profit by finding that spool of master tape. We need someone who was ruthless enough to have stabbed J.J. Fritch in the back, and we need above all someone who had access to the ice pick in the Bain house.

"Now, the selection of that weapon is an interesting thing. It means that the person who committed that murder wanted a weapon that would do the job, yet it wasn't the most efficient weapon on earth. It was a weapon that came to hand on the spur of the moment, say some time after midnight on the date of the murder.

"We need someone who could establish an alibi for an entire evening up to around 3:00 A.M., who had opportunity after that to go and kill Fritch, leave his body in the icebox until around eight in the morning and then plant it in some other place. Of course, finding the door of Brogan's apartment unlocked gave him the ideal place.

"So our murderer, Paul, is strong, ruthless, cold-blooded, scientific, interested in the fortunes of the Bain family and one who would have access to the ice pick."

"Good heavens," Della Street said, "do you realize that you're practically putting a rope around the neck of Jarrett Bain?"

Mason stood looking down at her and at the startled face of Paul Drake. He inhaled a deep drag from his cigarette, blew out the smoke, grinned and said, "Well?"

"Good Lord," Drake exclaimed, "when you look at it that way, it's the only possible solution. He came home and talked with his dad, he learned all about what you had said about the probability of the tape recording being forged, of it being spliced tape. Edison Doyle could give him an alibi for the time around two o'clock. Then he *said* he went to bed and slept until about ten o'clock. Good Lord!"

Mason said, "There was nothing whatever to have prevented him from going up to see J.J. Fritch around three-thirty in the morning, sticking an ice pick in Fritch's back, pulling the stuff out of the deep-freeze locker, putting Fritch in there, staying out until about eight o'clock in the morning, then going back and getting Fritch, putting him in the liquor closet where he knew the body would be discovered when Sylvia and I went to keep our nine o'clock appointment. Then he hastily dumped the food back into the icebox and—"

"Wait a minute," Paul Drake interposed, "you're narrowing the circle all right, but what about Edison Doyle? He was one who had to leave, and he was one who had an alibi for around midnight but didn't—"

"And look at the way he's built," Mason said. "Can you see *him* reaching down and picking J.J. Fritch up out of an icebox, carrying him across the hall and propping him in a liquor closet? Doyle is the fox-terrier type, but Jarrett Bain is a great, big, lumbering giant of a man with a bull neck, a huge pair of shoulders, and that peculiarly cold-blooded attitude of utter detachment which characterizes a certain type of scientist."

"So what are we going to do?" Paul Drake asked.

Mason turned to Della Street. "Ring up the Bain residence," he said. "See if you can get Jarrett Bain on the telephone."

Della Street put through the call, then after a moment looked at Mason with wide, startled eyes.

"What is it?" Mason asked.

"Jarrett isn't even going to be here for the funeral," she said. "He left word that he was sorry but he couldn't help the dead. He could only help the living. He said he'd received a wire on some new archaeological remains, and he took off by plane."

Mason pinched out his cigarette.

"Well," he said, "I guess he's gone, then. Do you know it might be a difficult matter to find him."

Drake seemed uncomfortable. "The police," he said, "are trying to pin this on Brogan. They're claiming the fingerprints are those of Brogan's accomplice, that Brogan engineered the whole thing."

Mason grinned.

"Aren't you going to tip them off," Della Street asked, "so that they can lay off of Brogan and catch Jarrett Bain before he disappears into the jungle?"

Mason grinned. "There is such a thing as poetic justice. Let's let Mr. Brogan sweat a little. They can't actually convict him on the evidence they have now. They have evidence enough to arrest but not enough to convict. As far as Jarrett Bain is concerned let's let the police solve their own problems.

"*Our* responsibilities are very definite and very limited, Della. We were representing Hattie Bain, who has now been discharged from custody."

"Hattie Bain and her green-eyed sister," Della said.

"Oh, by all means," Mason grinned, "the green-eyed sister. Little Miss Fix-It. We mustn't forget her!"

"Oh, my Lord!" Della Street exclaimed. "That telegram summoning Jarrett to the jungle on account of that new archaeological discovery! Remember she said—"

She broke off and looked wide-eyed at Perry Mason.

The lawyer lit another cigarette. "Little Miss Fix-It," he said.

ABOUT THE AUTHOR

Erle Stanley Gardner (1889–1970) was the top selling American author of the twentieth century, primarily due to the enormous success of his Perry Mason Mysteries, which numbered more than eighty and inspired a half-dozen motion pictures and radio programs, as well as a long-running television series starring Raymond Burr. Having begun his career as a pulp writer, Gardner brought a hard-boiled style and sensibility to his early Mason books, but he gradually developed into a more classic detective novelist, providing clues to allow astute readers to solve his many mysteries. For over a quarter of a century, he wrote more than a million words a year under his own name as well as numerous pseudonyms, the most famous being A. A. Fair.

THE PERRY MASON MYSTERIES

FROM MYSTERIOUSPRESS.COM
AND OPEN ROAD MEDIA

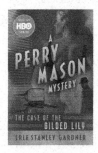

MYSTERIOUSPRESS.COM

Otto Penzler, owner of the Mysterious Bookshop in Manhattan, founded the Mysterious Press in 1975. Penzler quickly became known for his outstanding selection of mystery, crime, and suspense books, both from his imprint and in his store. The imprint was devoted to printing the best books in these genres, using fine paper and top dust-jacket artists, as well as offering many limited, signed editions.

Now the Mysterious Press has gone digital, publishing ebooks through **MysteriousPress.com**.

MysteriousPress.com offers readers essential noir and suspense fiction, hard-boiled crime novels, and the latest thrillers from both debut authors and mystery masters. Discover classics and new voices, all from one legendary source.

FIND OUT MORE AT
WWW.MYSTERIOUSPRESS.COM

FOLLOW US:
@emysteries and Facebook.com/MysteriousPressCom

MysteriousPress.com is one of a select group of publishing partners of Open Road Integrated Media, Inc.

THE MYSTERIOUS BOOKSHOP, founded in 1979, is located in Manhattan's Tribeca neighborhood. It is the oldest and largest mystery-specialty bookstore in America.

The shop stocks the finest selection of new mystery hardcovers, paperbacks, and periodicals. It also features a superb collection of signed modern first editions, rare and collectable works, and Sherlock Holmes titles. The bookshop issues a free monthly newsletter highlighting its book clubs, new releases, events, and recently acquired books.

58 Warren Street
info@mysteriousbookshop.com
(212) 587-1011
Monday through Saturday
11:00 a.m. to 7:00 p.m.

FIND OUT MORE AT:

www.mysteriousbookshop.com

FOLLOW US:

@TheMysterious and Facebook.com/MysteriousBookshop

OPEN ROAD

INTEGRATED MEDIA

Find a full list of our authors and
titles at www.openroadmedia.com

FOLLOW US
@OpenRoadMedia